His Purrfect Mate

Mating Heat - Book Two

By Laurann Dohner

His Purrfect Mate by Laurann Dohner

Shannon may be quarter puma, but can't shift. She's just a human with a few extra genes. But she knows how dangerous shifters are, and now she's their prey, captured by a group of werewolves for a deadly hunt. Then she's rescued by the biggest werewolf of them all. He's the sexiest male she's ever seen—jet-black hair, muscular body, piercing dark eyes and a growl that heats her blood.

Anton's body responds fervently to Shannon and he vows to protect her with his life—only to discover she's the enemy. As the future alpha of his pack, Anton knows a cat will never be accepted. There'll be hell to pay. But it's mating heat, and he's about to lose all control to that driving sexual need. His wolf wants her, can smell her desire. There's no way to stop it now—his animal won't be denied.

Dedication

To Mr. Laurann, for always being my hero.

Please note...

This book was originally put out a few years ago. It's a re-release. It's had some updated editing but I kept the original story intact.

Mating Heat Series

Mate Set

His Purrfect Mate

Mating Brand

His Purrfect Mate

Copyright © April 2016

Editor: Kelli Collins

Cover Art: Dar Albert

ISBN: 978-1-944526-11-5

Chapter One

Fear made Shannon's heart pound, her side burned from the pain of running, and she ducked just a tad too late. The tree branch snagged her long red hair, nearly jerking her off her feet, but she recovered, stumbled, and kept going. The sound of heavy pants and growls mingled with her ragged, harsh breathing.

I'm going to die, she thought, panicked. She forced her legs to keep pumping. Her bare feet stung from the cuts she could feel as she ran. The memory of telling her coworker just a week before that she hated the idea of turning thirty at the end of the month flittered through her thoughts. *Now I don't have to worry about it*, her mind whispered. *I'm not going to survive to celebrate my birthday.*

A twig snapped loudly to her left and she knew they were closing in for the kill. They could have taken her down by now, but instead they toyed with her, chased her through the thick woods, probably for the sheer joy of the hunt. How they'd found her or realized what she was remained a mystery.

This shouldn't have happened. Mom swore no one would ever suspect the truth.

Of course, that didn't put a screeching halt to the nightmare that had become her reality.

Two men had walked up to her as she'd been putting groceries in her car, punched her in the face, and she'd awoken into the middle of pure hell. They'd taken her shoes, her purse...and had given her a five-minute head start.

Howls filled the woods surrounding her. She saw a dark shape ahead and moved to avoid it, furiously wishing she had their speed and agility. She missed slamming in to another tree and the ground started to incline. She stumbled and fell, landing painfully on her knees. Both arms took the impact before her face could smash into the dirt. Dried leaves bit into her palms. She tried to lift up but her limbs shook from exhaustion.

A deep growl made her twist her head around and pure horror gripped her completely when the big black wolf stepped out of the thick foliage. Drool dripped from his open jaw, razor-sharp teeth revealed as he inched closer to her. The five feet separating them wasn't far enough.

Leaves crunched and she turned her head slowly in the direction of the sound, this time expecting the sight of the second wolf that appeared next to a big rock. A third one followed close on his tail. They growled, their intent to attack obvious.

Shannon panted, sweat trickling down her body, and her gaze lifted to the closest tree, which she nearly touched. She hoped the branch hung low enough for her to reach.

It took every ounce of her waning strength to surge to her feet and leap.

Her father had given her very few of his traits, but the one that might give her more time to live kicked in as her hands gripped the limb and her bare foot flattened on the bark. Something hairy brushed her other leg as she frantically climbed. Instinct and fear became a driving motivation for her not to look down, instead she grabbed at anything her fingers hooked onto. She kept going, even when the branches thinned dangerously and common sense told her to stop.

She finally hesitated when wood groaned. The wind blew and she swayed high in the treetops. A sick feeling knotted inside her stomach while she wondered if her weight would snap the branch she clung to, but then the wind died. Everything stilled except her pounding heartbeat. She stared down the far distance to the ground, another wave of fear flashing through her. Heights weren't her favorite thing.

Movement drew her attention and she watched as at least six wolves paced below, their heads tilted to glare up at her. She forced her lungs to hold air longer with each breath to slow her breathing and then scanned the area around. The distance between the trees was too great to hope she could transfer limb to limb to get away. They had her trapped on her perch high above them.

Howls sang out again and she shivered. More of them approached, and she realized just how outnumbered she was.

A loud groan jerked her attention back to the base of the tree. She gasped as one of the wolves started to transform. Horrified fascination widened her eyes while she witnessed fur recede into skin. The body shape changed more rapidly than she had imagined it could. She'd never seen it done until that moment.

The man had short blond hair and tan skin. He crouched on the ground for long seconds, recovering from the transformation, and then straightened. He looked up and she stared into the human features of a guy in his early twenties.

"Get down here," he demanded. "That's not fair."

Another one changed from wolf into man. She guessed him to be little more than a teenager, judging by his youthful appearance. Their nakedness didn't seem to bother them in the least as they stood shoulder to shoulder, the blond gawking up with a frown.

"Man, did you see how fast she climbed that tree? Why hasn't she changed?"

The blond shrugged. "I don't know and I don't care." He reached up for the first branch. "Get down here or I'll come up there after you."

Shannon had no words. The shock and horror of her circumstances still had her reeling. She licked her lips, forcing her brain to work. "Leave me alone! I've done nothing to you."

"You're the enemy." The blond paused. "For a chick, you're hot, but still, you know how it goes. You shouldn't have been walking around alone and unprotected. Maybe I'll fuck you before I kill you."

Talking wasn't going to get her out of this mess. They obviously didn't care that she'd never harmed them, hadn't sought them out, and they just wanted her dead because of who her father had been. She tried to remember his face but came up blank. No pictures had survived the fire that had taken his life just weeks after her fifth birthday.

More wolves suddenly ran into the small clearing and she counted eleven in all, including the two in skin. Werewolves were dreaded, vicious creatures, and they were sworn enemies of her father's people. Now that she had some time to think while she wasn't running for her life, she guessed they might have gone after her based on the misconception she was a full shifter. It probably wasn't her being a freak after all that had provoked them to attack but that didn't soothe her in the least. They would still tear her out of the tree and she would be slaughtered by the pack.

"That's just wrong to even joke about." The teen laughed. "Nobody is hard up enough to touch one of them. That's just sick, Donny."

"I knew you were gay," the blond, Donny, taunted. "I'd do her."

"I am not," the teen sputtered. "I guess we could have sex with her first."

Someone snorted loudly and another twenty-something male walked into Shannon's line of sight to peer up at her. "You're such a doofus, Milo. Have sex? Try saying you'll nail her." The naked guy grinned. "And yeah, she's a prime-looking pussy."

Shannon shivered with fear. "Leave me alone!"

A howl tore through the woods and the men started noticeably. The blond turned his head in the direction of the sound. "Shit. Anton is coming. He won't let us play with her first."

A really large black wolf entered the clearing. Shannon could tell even from far above that he had to be the biggest one of the bunch. He growled loud enough for her to tremble at the vicious sound. She watched him change back into his skin. It amazed her how fluid the transformation could be, how quickly it happened, and they weren't sobbing from the pain. She'd always assumed all that shifting bone and skin would hurt immensely.

The man was bigger than the others, even in human form. He had shoulder-length black hair and looked huge even from a good sixty feet above. He straightened to his feet and stretched, displaying dense muscles as he rolled his broad shoulders. He turned to face the three males standing under the tree.

"I told you to quit stalking these woods. You've almost killed off everything."

The blond hesitated. "We listened. We actually went out and found something outside our territory to hunt."

The big man put his hands on his bare hips. His ass and back teased Shannon's view but with the leaves on the branches, she couldn't see him really well. "That's not the point." He had a deep, scary voice. "I said to stop killing shit for a while. That doesn't mean go out and buy something to amuse yourselves. Do you have any idea how much it's going to cost my father to bring in enough animals to replenish all the ones you've killed? We're supposed to keep a low profile. Don't you think the locals will notice if they never see any deer or rabbits in the area?"

"But—"

"Enough," the larger man roared, his deep voice booming, and an eerie, disconcerting silence settled through the woods. The birds even grew quiet.

Time seemed to freeze and then the blond spoke. "We need to at least kill it first. We can't let it go."

"Bullshit," the man rumbled. "Go home."

"What if she tells someone what we did to her? It could bring our pack some trouble if her family gets pissed off."

The big man's head jerked up and Shannon stopped breathing when a handsome face peered at her. He had strong masculine features and his dark eyes widened when his gaze met hers. His mouth parted, his shock clear—and then a roar of outrage tore from his parted lips.

Shannon trembled, her terror returning fiercely, and she almost lost her tight grip on the branch she clung to.

The man below her moved fast. His arm shot out and he punched the blond, knocking him a good six feet, where he struck the ground and sprawled on his back.

"Run," he snarled, "before I kill the lot of you worthless assholes."

The blond struggled to his feet, a red mark visible on his face from the bloody wound the striking fist had left, and then everyone fled, wolves and men in skin.

The dark-haired stranger remained. He stood unmoving and then slowly tilted his head up again, his dark, angry gaze on Shannon once more.

Anton battled his inner rage. If he didn't get control of it quickly, he'd shift out of his skin and go after the pups who had treed a woman. He really wanted to tear up their hides, make them suffer, but he couldn't do that. He had a situation to handle first.

His mind immediately added up obvious facts. The pups had grabbed a woman, hunted her, and now she'd become *his* problem.

If he'd known of her presence, he never would have shifted. She had a bird's-eye view of the clearing, he felt certain she'd seen him transform into his skin, and he had no idea how to fix this cluster-fuck of a mess.

He watched her with a sense of dismay. He didn't want to kill her but she had seen too much. His father would have a fit if he allowed her to leave the woods alive. It really would bring hell to the pack if she were able to go to the police.

On second thought, they'd probably think she had to be a major nutcase if she babbled about werewolves.

He bit his lip, debated, and finally decided he could never kill a woman.

He cleared his throat, not sure what to say, but knew his first problem would be talking her down out of the tree. He feared she'd panic if he tried to climb up to her and she might fall to her death. She had managed to ascend high enough that the branches had thinned, putting her in danger of a limb snapping from her weight. Her small-looking body appeared to be wrapped tightly around a branch.

"You can come down. I promise you're safe now."

She licked her lips. "Go away and I'll climb down when you're gone."

He hesitated, wishing it could be that simple. "I'll escort you to your car or return you to your campground—wherever they chased you from. I swear I won't hurt you. I realize you're in shock but no harm will befall you as long as I'm around."

She shook her head, her red hair snaking around her body to her waist. "Just go away. Shooo!"

Amusement surprised him. "Did you just 'shoo' me?"

The woman hesitated. "I've done nothing to you or to them."

14

He watched her turn her head to glance around the area and rage returned instantly upon seeing the dark bruise along her jawline. Someone had clocked her with a fist. She had very pale skin, and appeared to be smaller than average. He decided his pups were in for a beating of monumental proportions when he got his hands on them for what they'd done to the woman.

"I know you're in shock and I realize you must be very frightened, but I swear you're safe now. I'm Anton." He paused, regretting giving her his name but it had just slipped out. "I'm afraid that branch is going to snap and you'll fall to your death if it does. Please come down."

"I'm not stupid. You're trying to trick me."

He didn't blame her for her fear or suspicion. She had to be traumatized as hell. Not only had she been attacked and hunted, but learning werewolves really existed after watching them change forms had to be messing up her human mind. He took a slow breath and blew it out. It didn't help his case that he stood there completely naked. She probably feared him because he not only turned into a wolf, but he might also be some major pervert who'd attack her.

"I don't think you're stupid. They were really wrong to attack you. I sent them away but that doesn't mean others aren't out running in the woods. If I left and you tried to walk out on your own, to be honest, there's a real possibility that you'd run into more of them. I understand you don't know me but you saw me chase

15

them off. You watched me strike one of them when I realized what they'd done to you. I give you my word—I won't harm you or allow anyone else to."

"You could be a big fat liar."

"I could be." He hid a smile, amused again. She had a nice voice, and as he studied her, that wasn't the only thing he could appreciate. Most of her face remained hidden by a curtain of hair, but from what he could see, she appeared pretty. "You're right. Let me put it this way. How long do you think you could survive up in that tree? It'll grow dark soon and the temperatures will drop drastically. Do you really want to spend a cold, miserable night up there? I doubt you want to climb down and stumble around in the dark once I leave. You also can't stay up there indefinitely. It would only be a matter of time before you either have to climb down or they climb up after you, if more of them are in the woods. At this moment, you've got no chance of survival, but I'm offering you safety and protection."

She seemed to mull over his words. Anton watched her pull her lower lip into her mouth and then the pouty fuller lip returned after she bit it or sucked on it. He wished he could see more of her features but her messy hair hid too much.

"Okay. But I want you to swear on your life that you won't hurt me, or allow them to."

"I give you my word of honor and that means everything to me," he stated honestly, relaxing. The faster he got her back to her world, the quicker he could get on with his day—after he kicked some pup ass. "I'll protect you with my life."

She moved and Anton received another surprise. She'd been balled up, wrapped tightly around the thin branch, in a fetal position. As she lowered her legs and stretched downward toward a branch, he saw a glimpse of her shape. She didn't appear very big but what he *could* see had definite appeal to him as a man. Werewolf women tended to be tall but on the lean side. The woman had a lush body with soft curves.

"What's your name?"

She paused on her downward climb to twist her head and peer at him. "Shannon."

He didn't comment, or blame her for not sharing her last name. Neither had he. If she reported the attack to the police, he didn't want them to have too much information. The last thing he needed would be bullshit questions from some overworked cop who wouldn't see the humor in checking out a woman's crazy tale of a werewolf attack. He pulled away from his musings to watch her climb lower.

Anger returned when he saw blood smeared on her bare feet and he stopped breathing through his nose. The scent of her blood so soon after he'd shifted could affect him. The last thing the woman needed would be to see his eyes darken or hear his voice thicken into growls.

He pulled air in through his mouth and hoped the scent wouldn't be strong enough to taste. The cologne he always splashed on before pack meetings would help mask it. He'd made a habit of wearing the stuff to keep some details of his personal life private. Wolves could smell way too much but artificial fragrances could confuse their noses.

He moved under her, ready to assist as she climbed down the tree.

"That's it," he encouraged. "Don't fall, Shannon. I'm going to reach up and help you down, okay? Don't be alarmed because I'm not wearing clothes. I swear I won't hurt you."

She paused again to shoot him a frightened look. He could make out more of her features, and his gut tightened. She had big, beautiful blue eyes framed with dark eyelashes, and they were shaped in a way that stole his breath away. Not even the purplish bruise could distract from her attractiveness. He hesitated and then lifted his arms to assist her to the ground.

"It's okay, Shannon." He kept his tone soft, attempting to lure her closer to safety. "I keep my word. No one is going to hurt you."

Anton could tell she wasn't certain if he could be trusted but she still lowered down the last eight feet that separated them until he gently gripped her waist. His hands wrapped around soft hips and he tried not to notice her full, rounded ass displayed in the pair of thin cotton capri pants too close to his face. He really didn't want to become aroused. She'd scream if he allowed his body to show his sexual interest.

He lifted her easily, placing her carefully on the ground. She turned, faced him, and kept her gaze fused with his. She didn't glance down at his body but instead gave him a fearful look that made him wonder if she'd attempt to climb the tree again. Her back pressed tightly against the bark. He could see her terror as clearly as the cute, tiny freckles sprinkled across the bridge of her nose. Her much shorter height—a few inches above five feet—made him question her age. She looked mature, late twenties maybe, but then again, teens seemed to appear much older than their years, in his opinion.

"See? I'm not going to hurt you." He tried to sound harmless, the irony of that not lost on him since he had to be the most dangerous thing within miles of the small female. "I'm the good guy," he lied. No one would ever call Anton Harris that title without it being the punch line of a sarcastic joke. He had become one of the most feared members of his pack. "Where did you come from? I'll take you back there."

Fear gripped Shannon in such an emotionally tight fist that it made breathing difficult. She knew she couldn't hide it from him. A big, vicious werewolf in his human shape of solid muscle and strength stood just feet from her. He had to be at least six-four. She regretted climbing out of the tree. Her instincts screamed at her to

19

flee but her legs refused to move. They were rooted to the ground — heavy and paralyzed.

"Hey," he whispered, his deep voice turning husky. "Calm down, Shannon. It's going to be fine."

Her mouth opened but nothing came out. She wondered if this gripping terror came from the same part of her she'd thought she'd gotten a handle on years before. Memories surfaced of her childhood, of those gut reactions she sometimes experienced, that other part of her she chalked up to her father's diluted but rare bloodline.

In the third grade, a bully had pushed her. She'd hissed at him and clawed his arm, not meaning to, but it just happened. In fifth grade, she'd found herself up a tree when a dog had run at her. She couldn't remember how she'd gotten up there or even making the decision to do it, but somehow she'd discovered her ability to climb pretty much anything if fear motivated her. Her teen years had been a nightmare when the urge to eat raw meat had struck with puberty. She'd feared, along with her mother, that it meant more than it had. But she'd never changed, never done any of the other things her father could, and the fear had eventually passed.

"Where do you live? Let's start with that."

His voice drew her from her childhood confusion and she stared into the darkest eyes she'd ever seen. They were framed with thick, long eyelashes that matched his jet-black hair. He didn't look at her in a way that justified her fear but it still remained in full force. She knew she had to find her voice to answer him.

"Anderson," she got out. "I live there."

His full lips curved downward. "That's a distance from here. What were you doing taking a stroll in the woods?"

"I wasn't." Talking became easier. "I was taken from the grocery store parking lot two blocks from my apartment. That blond you hit and another guy walked up to me. The blond's friend punched me in the face and I woke here."

He closed his eyes and the anger that tensed his features made Shannon push tighter against the massive tree, wishing she could climb back up it, even inside it, to hide from the large wolf in skin. He softly growled before his eyes snapped open again.

"I'll make them pay for this, okay? The important part is, I found you in time." He paused. "If you tell anyone about this, they won't believe it. Are you aware of that? I don't want them locking you up in some loony bin. You've been through enough without that shit. I'll get you home and you need to forget this ever happened, okay?"

She nodded, acknowledging the intelligence of his advice. The cops would put her into a straightjacket if she told them the truth. Worse, it would draw attention to her, a really bad thing, and something she'd always feared.

He relaxed. "Good. If it makes you feel any better, I'm going to beat the hell out of those boys for kidnapping you. They won't move for weeks without regretting ever putting a finger on you."

Shannon saw sincerity as he spoke and some of her fear eased. His anger wasn't directed at her but at the ones who'd attacked her. She could happily deal with that. All she wanted now was to get away from him and go home. She silently promised to move out of her apartment as soon as possible. If they'd found her, someone else could too. She loved her home but she preferred remaining alive a lot more.

They both tensed when a twig snapped nearby. Their heads jerked toward the direction of the sharp sound. Shannon tried to spin around and lunge up the tree when a wolf came into view. Terror overtook everything else, but a big strong hand grabbed her arm to keep her tethered. She started to shake as the wolf growled viciously and his body lowered into a crouching position, preparing to pounce on her.

Shannon clawed at the hand holding her still, a scream trapped inside her throat, but Anton wouldn't let go. She heard him snarl at the wolf, maybe even at her; she wasn't sure where he directed his anger. She was too panic-stricken to do anything but try to flee.

"Enough!" Anton roared. "Jerry, back off. You're terrifying her."

She couldn't break free of the hold on her arm and she couldn't get up the tree. She needed to climb, needed to get higher, out of the wolf's reach, and her instincts screamed in a painful blast of strong awareness.

She spun, faced Anton, and before she could stop herself, grabbed him. Her hand gripped his shoulder and she jumped, her body hitting his much larger one. To her horror, she wrapped around him, clinging to his body with every ounce of strength she had. Her legs squeezed around his waist and her face burrowed into his neck.

Shock held Anton immobile as the woman trembled against his chest. Her arm wound tighter around his neck, nearly strangling him, as her legs locked around his waist and her heels dug into the muscles of his ass. Her breathing tickled as she panted against his neck. He had to move his head to see Jerry since her long, tangled red hair partially covered his face and then he glared at his pack mate.

He released her upper arm after a slight hesitation to wrap both of his around her waist, hugging her. She trembled harder when her other arm wrapped around his neck and a protective feeling spurred his anger to burn brighter at the wolf sitting in the clearing staring at him with a dazed, confused look.

"It's okay." He tried to comfort Shannon. "I ordered you to take off, Jerry. You're scaring her."

The wolf lowered his head and changed form. It irritated Anton but he couldn't stop the other man from what he'd already started to do. When Jerry pushed up to his feet, he gawked at Anton and the woman in astonishment.

"What the hell are you doing with a *cat* wrapped around you?"

A cat? Anton inhaled through his nose, trying to filter the scent of her blood from the scent of the cloying cologne that hindered his usually acute sense of smell. The scents of her nearly overwhelmed him. Vanilla mixed with pure terror, woman, strawberries, and...

"Fuck," he groaned, tensing. "You're a shifter. No wonder they hunted you."

Shannon quaked harder, clung more frantically, and he realized something important.

She wasn't hurting him. No teeth tore into his exposed jugular where her lips pressed against his neck. Her fingernails dug into his shoulders but they weren't claws. Even her strength wasn't nearly what it should be as a shifter. He had no doubt she held on to him as tightly as she could while her adrenaline pumped, but he could throw her off with minimum effort.

Anton's instincts started to kick in while he inhaled more of her scent, the identity of her shifter blood becoming known, and his wolf didn't enjoy it. He growled but didn't toss her away or crush the life from her inside the cage of his arms. He could have done either.

"Puma," Jerry confirmed. "Weak though. I barely picked up her smell when I got close. I came to investigate who would be stupid enough to trespass into our territory. I guess you get to kill her instead of me."

Shannon whimpered in his arms and Anton softly growled. He'd promised her safety, swore to protect her, and he always kept his word. For some reason, she trusted him to do so. He took a few steadying breaths and used every trick he'd ever learned to get a grip on his wolf so it didn't hurt the woman he held. He finally relaxed.

"I'm not going to kill her," he stated clearly. "Go get me some clothes, and I need my truck to drive her home."

Jerry's jaw dropped and then he growled. Anger tightened his features and the wolf flashed in his eyes. "Kill her. She's our enemy."

Anton snarled back, glaring. "I gave you an order. Go, or *you're* going to be the one to die."

Chapter Two

Shannon calmed but it took time. It embarrassed her that she couldn't seem to control her reactions. Big, warm hands rubbed her from shoulder to waist, up and down, over and over, gently. It helped her fear recede until she finally loosened her death grip on him.

"That's it," Anton whispered. "Easy, kitten. Nobody is going to hurt you."

She trembled again and finally lifted her face away from his neck. He turned his head and their gazes met. He stopped petting her and took a deep breath, pushing firmly against her body when his lungs expanded.

"You're not a teenager."

She shook her head.

That drew a frown from him. "I'm trying to understand why you didn't shift when they hunted you, or when you could have attacked me."

She just stared into his dark gaze. Her fear returned and her body tensed.

"Easy." His tone lowered. "I'm not going to hurt *you* and you're not going to hurt *me*."

She couldn't wound him if she tried, and that was the problem. She finally looked away from his intense dark eyes to study his masculine features—wide cheekbones, straight nose, and generous lips. He needed to shave, a little bit of dark beard shadowed his jawline and upper lip. It could have been a lingering effect after his transformation, since he appeared to have more than a little Native American ancestry. His silky black hair fell to his shoulders, all one length, parted down the center. Her gaze returned to his.

"You could have gotten away. I've gone after your kind before and I know how fast you can run. Why didn't you? Toying with a bunch of wolves isn't overly bright, and you look old enough to know better."

Shannon had to clear the lump in her throat before she could speak. "I can't," she whispered.

He frowned, deep lines marring the area around his mouth. "You can't what?"

Fear of sharing the truth with him made her pause. She didn't know werewolf customs or beliefs. She had been assured that her father's family would consider her an abomination, something that shouldn't be. Had his family known about her, and had they been given the chance, they'd have killed her at birth.

"You can't what? Be intelligent?" His eyebrow rose.

"Shift," she admitted.

He blinked, his frown melted away, and surprise registered on his features. "Are you that injured?" He sniffed. "I smell blood on you but not a lot."

"Do you still promise not to hurt me?"

"I always keep my word."

Again, he seemed sincere. Her tongue darted out to wet her dry lips. His gaze followed the movement before lifting back to meet her eyes when she spoke.

"My mother is human, and my father was only half puma from having a human father."

The handsome man studied her carefully. "Shit. You're more human than puma. You really can't shift?"

She shook her head.

"No claws or teeth?"

She released him with one arm and held up her hand, showed him her fingernails, and then pulled back her upper lip to display her normal teeth. "I'm terrified," she admitted, curling her fingers around the hot skin at the curve of his shoulder. "If I could, I'd have done it by now."

"You scent of shifter but it's very faint."

"I didn't know that."

"Your father didn't tell you?"

Shannon hesitated again, wondered what he'd do if he realized she had no one to protect her, and no one to avenge her if he broke his word. No worried shifter family would look for her or care if he dumped her dead body into the nearest ravine.

"I asked you a question and I expect an answer." He adjusted his hold on her, one arm sliding under her ass to lift her a little higher until their faces were level while he peered into her eyes. "He didn't warn you that other shifters could detect you're part puma?"

"No." *That is the truth,* she mentally admitted.

"He should watch out for you better. I've heard your males are really protective of their women. I'm not picking up a male scent on you so I assume you don't have a mate?"

"No mate."

"You're sure old enough for one. Is it because you're defective?"

Some of her fear left to be replaced by anger. A lifetime of being deemed a freak haunted her, and had her on the defense. "Are *you* mated?"

"No."

"You're sure old enough. Are you defective too?"

The arm tightened around her waist and a soft growl rumbled from his parted lips. "Careful, kitten. Don't insult me."

Fear flashed inside her and it cooled her temper. She wasn't lipping off to just some random guy. This was a real werewolf.

"You insulted me first. You should have seen the look on your face, the disbelief, and you smirked."

"Did I?" His mouth twitched and humor lit his dark gaze. "It surprised me." His attention lingered on her mouth, slid to her hair, and then returned to stare deeply into her eyes. "You're attractive as hell."

Mute again, she had no idea how to respond to that, never expecting a compliment from him. He took another deep breath, watched her, and then cocked his head.

"Someone is coming. Are you calm enough now for me to put you down without you trying to climb the nearest tree, or me, again?"

"I don't know. My instincts kind of take over when I'm super scared and then it's a blur until I find myself in bad places, like at the top of a tree." She glanced down at his broad chest. "You're the first man I ever climbed, if that helps any, but you wouldn't let me go, in my defense. Something inside me wanted off the ground."

"Instincts can be a bitch." He turned his head slightly to peer into the woods. "Hang on to me then. You're about to be terrified. Four of my pack mates are approaching."

He moved when she buried her face against his skin again, closed her eyes, and wrapped both arms around his neck to hold on tightly once more. Her back gently brushed the trunk of the tree she'd abandoned and he pinned her there, inside his embrace. She heard leaves crunch nearby and sucked in Anton's masculine scent. For some strange reason, it helped her not freak out when the first growl of alarm sounded once his pack mates saw or smelled her.

"That's far enough." Anton's voice came out deep and commanding, harsh. "Go home."

"Cat," a male snarled. He growled louder. "Toss her this way. I want a bite. She smells sweet."

Anton's entire body stiffened. He felt similar to the tree trunk pressed against her backside. The terrifying snarl of rage near her left ear had her holding back a whimper. Instincts flared to life again and it took every bit of concentration not to struggle to get out of his arms. She wanted to run or climb a tree, but definitely not be in that clearing near a werewolf who wanted to make a snack out of her.

"Back off," Anton roared. "Mine!"

"Fuck," another voice grumbled. "What happened to sharing a fresh kill?"

"Whoa," another male gasped. "I don't think that's what he's got in mind for her. Shit. Sorry man. I know you like pussy but hell, that's as literal as it gets."

One of the werewolves snorted. "You're going to fuck her and then kill her? I'm an admitted asshole but that's harsh even for me."

"Leave," Anton snarled, his voice a terrifying sound.

31

"Okay," one of them muttered. "Tell me how it is later. You're the man, Anton. Really. I wouldn't let one of them near me. Watch her teeth and claws or she's going to tear you apart."

They retreated and Shannon's fear eased when the man pinning her relaxed and stepped away from the tree until her back wasn't touching it any longer. She lifted her head and saw anger still etched on his features. He breathed a little heavily but then his gaze softened when he stared at her.

"Jerry will bring me clothes and he'll have driven my truck closer. He'll park it not too far from here. I'll get dressed and take you home."

She hesitated. "They stole my purse. My keys, identification, and money are inside it."

Irritation flashed on his handsome face. "I'll get it back and make sure they didn't take a dime from you."

"Thank you." She meant it.

"I'm going to have to call your father and smooth things out with him. I don't want this starting a war between our people."

A new sliver of fear sliced through her. "That's okay. Don't worry about it. I won't tell him what happened."

"He's going to know the second you walk in the door. He'll smell me all over you and your terror is really strong. I take it you didn't inherit a keen sense of smell? You reek of it."

"I live alone."

Dark eyes narrowed and he studied her. "You do?"

"Yes. I'll shower when I get home and clean my clothes." She paused. "I'm sorry I smell." The guy was hot, he said she stank, and she hated that he had to be the best-looking guy she'd ever been that close to. She inwardly winced at that little bit of life's irony.

The silence grew uncomfortable between them and Shannon had to look away from his intense gaze, wondering why he stared at her in that odd manner. It was as if he were trying to read her mind. Her legs around his waist started to ache and she relaxed a little, her body slipping down his torso a bit.

His hands suddenly slid from their hold on her waist to cup her ass, and he lifted her higher.

Shannon gasped. "Do you want to let my butt go?"

"If you slide any lower it's going to embarrass one of us. I'm holding you up, that's all."

"Embarrass?"

His Adam's apple bobbed as he swallowed hard. "Fear turns me on—and so do you."

It took a few seconds for his words to translate into meaning inside her brain. Shocked, she twisted, her head swiveling enough to glance over her shoulder and down their bodies. The movement pressed her lower half tighter against his stomach but she got a glimpse of verification that one turned-on male held her. The sight made her snap back around and her hair slapped him in the face. She gaped at him.

Anton blew her hair away from his mouth and one eyebrow arched. "You had to look, huh?"

Heat flushed her cheeks. "You can put me down."

"I'd rather hold you until Jerry returns with my clothes. I don't want to have to talk you down from the tree again after you've admitted to me that you have a tendency to climb when you're afraid. You were about to tell me why you live alone. Don't think I can be distracted. I want an answer."

The glimpse she'd gotten of the guy's lower region had shaken her. The reason for his strong grip on her ass, to keep her from sliding down, had been impossible to miss. He had a major hard-on. The sight had triggered her fear of him again. The guy was big all over.

"Do *you* live with someone?"

His frown deepened, creating faint lines around his mouth. "No. I'm also not an unmated, attractive female. Stop stalling and explain why you aren't protected."

"I am," she lied. "I just enjoy having my own apartment."

A soft rumble of a growl came from his throat. Shannon tensed and her hands gripped his bare shoulders a little more firmly. Fear inched up her spine at the irritated expression he gave her.

"I'm not totally ignorant of you felines or your ways. Your family would keep you close to make sure your males didn't force you to mate with one of them. If you were ugly, I'd chalk it up to none of your men being interested, but I don't buy that for a second. If you were in my pack, the males would break down your door to get to you if you lived alone. Answer the question *now* and stop bullshitting me."

Her heart sped up from fear but he obviously wasn't going to let it go. He'd sworn not to hurt her, hadn't so far, and she decided to be honest. "Okay. My father died in a fire and his family doesn't know about me." She lifted her chin defiantly. "I take care of myself."

"Why don't they know about you? You need to get in contact with them. Do you know anything about shifters?" Shock widened his eyes. "You need to be protected. It's a miracle one of your males hasn't forced you to take him as a mate. You're not strong enough to defend yourself against any asshole who wants you. Your family would make sure you ended up with a guy you wanted to be with."

"I've never met another of my kind," she admitted softly. Her shoulders shrugged. "They don't live in this area. My mom moved us here to avoid them on purpose."

"Why?"

Nerves caused her mouth to go dry. She wanted to look anywhere but at him. Instead, she forced her gaze to stay with his. "They'd kill me."

35

"No, they wouldn't."

"Yes, they would." She sighed. "My father had to flee from his family, and he knew if they found us, we'd die. His mother helped him escape when their leader realized my father's human blood diluted his abilities. They hate weakness, and they kill for it. He could shift—my mother told me how beautiful he looked when he did—but I can't take another form. If they thought *he* was weak..." Her voice trailed off, allowing him to draw his own conclusions.

"Shit," he whispered. "I didn't realize how vicious cats were. When we have weak-blooded ones, we tend to just protect them more."

"When I was young, my father swore I smelled completely human. My mom promised me that I'd be safe and no one would ever know my heritage."

"When did you lose your father?"

"Just after my fifth birthday."

"When you hit puberty, did anything change with you? Sometimes that can trigger it with mixed breeds."

"I started craving raw meat. Mom took me into the woods to see if I could shift but it didn't happen, no matter how hard I tried."

His hands on her ass tightened, adjusting her a little in his hold. "Fear would have triggered it as well. You can't shift. I assumed you were younger until I got a closer look at your face. Some female teens have problems until puberty is over. The only other things that would prevent you from shifting are severe injury or drugs."

"I guess that's useful to know but it doesn't do me any good."

He blinked a few times. "Your scent obviously changed. You smell of puma, your father's breed, but it's faint. Any shifter could pick it up if they were within a few dozen yards of you. Can you pick up my scent?"

She inhaled. "You're wearing cologne, and whatever you wash your hair with smells kind of fruity."

"That's all you smell?"

She hesitated and then dropped her gaze to his throat. She leaned in, noticed when he instinctively jerked back a little, but then he held his body still, allowing her near his neck. Her nose hovered very close to his skin while she took another sniff.

Shannon couldn't detect much except for his cologne. It held a musky, wonderful aroma. She wasn't able to pick up whatever he thought she should be able to smell. She tried again, this time brushing her nose along his skin to get a stronger scent. The hands gripping her tightened as he pulled her against his stomach more firmly.

Her head lifted and she stared into his eyes. "You smell nice but just the way a normal guy does to me."

A soft sound came from his throat, not a growl, but close. "If you lick me to test my taste, you're going to be in a world of trouble."

His statement confused Shannon. "Why would I do that? Do shifters do that…taste people?"

The sound he made became clearer as he did it again, only louder. He groaned and turned his head, scanning the forest. "Come on, Jerry. Where the hell are you?" His hands relaxed on her ass.

Shannon decided he looked uncomfortable. "What's wrong?"

His dark, beautiful eyes fixed on her. "Foreplay, kitten. That's what you just initiated, but you have no idea, do you?"

Surprise shot her eyebrows up. "Really? Just sniffing at you?"

"Yeah. You're wrapped around me too."

"You could put me down."

"And you could end up adorning the tree again. No. Jerry will come. We'll just stay this way until then."

"I'll hold your hand. I'm much calmer and I'm starting to trust you. I think I can resist the urge to leave the ground if I'm close to you."

"If I put you down, you're going to get a better view of me."

Heat crept back into her cheeks. He didn't need to expand on that. She said nothing but silently urged Jerry to come back with

38

clothes for Anton. She dropped her attention to his chest, again noticing how broad and muscular he was.

"I take it you've never had sex with a shifter?"

"No." She refused to meet his eyes, stunned he'd ask her such a personal question. "I told you, I've never run into another one."

"That's a good thing. You aren't strong at all. That's why I thought you were human at first."

She met his gaze again. "I'm mostly human."

"You are." He turned his head, examined the woods, and smiled tightly. "Here he comes. Don't be afraid. He's not going to hurt you."

Jerry had put on a T-shirt, jeans, and a pair of dirty sneakers. He walked into the clearing with Anton's clothes hooked over one arm and keys dangled from his hand. The grin on his face spread.

"Did I interrupt?" Amusement laced his voice. "It looks as though I did." He chuckled. "I see things are getting real hard around here."

"Shut up, drop the clothes, the keys, and get lost," Anton grumbled.

"You could hand her over to me." Jerry moved closer. "We could share her. I'm past the urge to kill her but she sure is a pretty thing. I can think of at least five things I'd enjoying doing to her body."

"You would lose a hand if you touch her. She's under my protection and this isn't what you think."

"You obviously want to nail her, so what's stopping you?" Jerry halted in his tracks. "I'm wondering if they mewl when they're getting fucked?"

"Keep wondering and keep on going." Anton's voice deepened. "Go."

"Fine." The other man dropped the clothes and keys, spun on his heel, and headed back into the woods. "It's probably a good thing if you don't screw her. Your mother would rather see you castrated than hook up with a cat."

Anger appeared to have Anton seething. Shannon studied his features and fear crept back when he glared at her, giving her his full attention after his pack mate disappeared. His eyes had changed slightly, the shape of them noticeably different, and the hair along his jawline and upper lip looked suspiciously longer to her.

"Your face," she whispered.

"I'm angry. Sorry." He took deep breaths, the changes disappearing until he looked one-hundred-percent human. "It's easier to lose control right after a shift. The longer you stay in skin, the easier it is to keep it."

"Oh."

His hands tightened on her but then he adjusted his hold, forcing her to release him with her legs when he pushed her away from his torso. Shannon gasped but stood. The quick view of a naked, aroused Anton left her holding her breath before he spun away. The guy had a well-proportioned body, big *all* over, and she couldn't help but stare at his rounded, firm ass when he bent to retrieve the clothes.

He dressed quickly in a pair of black sweatpants and a navy tank top, keeping his back to her the entire time. He turned to face her after he had covered his body, his erection still visible since his friend hadn't bothered to bring him underwear. Shannon jerked her gaze up, trying not to gawk at the tented pants.

"Let's go. My boots will be with the truck. I'll have to return your purse at a later date but I *will* get it back to you."

"I won't be able to get into my apartment if I don't have my keys, and my car is still in the parking lot of the grocery store. I need to—"

"Get the hell away from me before I do something stupid," he grumbled. "You said an apartment? Don't you have a manager with a spare key?"

"Yes." She hadn't thought of that. Shannon nodded. "I even have a spare set of car keys at home. I locked my set inside once and it costs a small bundle to have someone come out to pop the lock."

"Let's go, kitten."

"My name is *Shannon*. Why do you keep calling me that?"

Anton gave her his back as he walked away. "It's a reminder to me, so I don't forget that dogs and cats don't mix well." He strode quickly through the woods. "Keep up."

Shannon followed. Her feet hurt, but she didn't complain. Anton had saved her from his pack, protected her, and kept his word. She wasn't going to ask him to carry her through the woods on top of all he'd already done. Though as she stared at his broad back, she felt certain the strong guy could easily do it.

Chapter Three

Shannon fought back hot tears. Her arms hugged her chest and the police officer who stood next to her cleared his throat, demanding her attention. She turned her head to stare at him.

"Who would do this, Miss Alvers? Do you have an angry ex-boyfriend? Maybe a new boyfriend with an ex-girlfriend who didn't want to let him go?"

"No." She winced over the destroyed couch and the way the guts of it had been spread across the room as if it had snowed cotton filling. "I don't date."

The cop gave her a disbelieving glance. "Look, lying isn't an option here. Someone has a lot of rage directed toward you. They tore up all your furniture, broke your tables, and shredded most of your clothes. Whoever did this is dangerous. You need to give us a name. Who's the guy?"

"There's no guy in my life." She faced him, hugging her waist tighter. "My last boyfriend moved to Oklahoma three years ago." She didn't mention how horrible that relationship had ended or how he'd accused her of being insane. Dating hadn't ever worked out for her in long-term relationships. "Last I heard, he got married and had a child. The guy before him had to be five or six years ago. He joined the Army and I have no idea where he is now. We both decided it would be best to break up."

"You date women?"

"No," she huffed. "Is it really so hard to believe I don't date?"

The cop gave her a once-over again, his gaze traveling up and down her body. "Yes, it is. You're an attractive woman."

"I have sex toys, a body pillow to cuddle with, and a heating blanket to keep me warm at night. They don't borrow money they never pay back, don't think I'm weird for any of my habits they don't agree with, and they don't argue with me."

The officer's mouth dropped open and Shannon blushed, realizing what she'd just sputtered. That was another reason she didn't date anymore. She had spent so much time alone as a child that she'd never learned to hold her tongue when she grew angry or upset. She just spoke her mind. Words left her mouth before she could halt them.

"You asked. I answered." She looked away from him. "I don't know who would do this. I'd tell you if I even had a guess. I can't afford to replace any of this and I don't have renter's insurance."

"Move," a male voice demanded loudly.

In seconds a big body filled the doorway and Shannon gaped at the man she never thought she'd see again.

Anton wore a black leather jacket that hung open a few inches to reveal a heavy-metal T-shirt. His hair had been pulled back in a ponytail. A pair of furious dark eyes locked on her.

44

"What happened here? I pulled up and saw the cop car." He glanced away from her and quickly scanned the room. "Damn." He sniffed and then sneezed. He jerked his gaze back to hers. "Are you hurt?"

The cop sauntered toward Anton. "Who are you?"

Anton didn't budge except to put his hands on his hips. "I'm a friend of hers. Shannon? Answer me now. Were you here when this happened? Did anyone hurt you?"

"No. I got a call from a neighbor who'd already called the police after they heard someone breaking things inside my apartment. I came home to find it this way."

"Who are you?" The officer grabbed Anton's arm.

Shannon tensed, wondering what she should do, if anything. She feared the werewolf would attack the cop.

Anton glared at the hand on his arm and then slowly reached into his back pocket, withdrew his wallet, and flipped it open to show his license. "I'm Anton Harris. I'm a friend of the family. I stopped by to drop off Shannon's purse. She left it inside my truck the other night when I drove her home. She can't hold her liquor worth shit and I was the designated driver."

The cop released him, turned, and glowered at Shannon. "Is *this* your boyfriend?"

"No. You heard him. He's a friend of my family. I've known him for years," she lied. She kept eye contact with the cop, hoping he'd believe her.

"Fine." The cop sighed. "I think I'm done here." He wrote something on a card and handed it to Shannon. "Here's the number for the case and my business card. Contact me if you discover anything has been stolen." He left quickly.

Shannon stared at Anton, watching him frown as he took inventory of every inch of the destroyed room. He finally faced her, still looking grim.

"A shifter did this."

Surprise jolted through her. "How do you know that?"

"Smell the bleach? It's to mask their scent."

"I just figured they spilled it from the bottle in the kitchen."

"You were wrong. Have you contacted your father's people?"

"No."

"Then mine did this." He walked through the living room and disappeared into her bedroom.

Shannon hesitated and then followed him, stepping over her broken coffee table. Her room had been tossed, her clothes strewn around, and her bed had been shredded and the dresser drawers pulled out. Anton stood in the middle of her small sleeping space. He turned to meet her gaze.

"Why would a shifter do this?"

Broad, leather-clad shoulders shrugged. "A few of them may be resentful after the beat-down they received for attacking you. They had your purse and access to your address. I guess they didn't believe me when I warned them that you were under my protection."

She forced her stunned gaze from his angry one, bent down, and flinched over discovering her favorite jacket sliced up. At first she thought someone had used a knife to do the damage but upon closer inspection, she guessed it could have been done with sharp claws, judging by the spacing of the tears.

"I'm sorry."

She lifted her chin, seeing sincerity in his eyes. "I'd planned on moving but I need to wait for my next paycheck. I don't exactly make enough money to keep a savings account so I don't have anything on hand for an emergency."

"I'll pay for this."

He shocked her again. "Why?"

"My pups, my responsibility, and trust me, they are going to pay me back every dime." He sighed, glancing around her room. "You can't stay here."

"I get paid Monday. I'm sure they won't come back. They ruined everything so it's not as if there's anything left to damage."

Anton had promised to protect her and he'd failed. He could pick up scents inside the bedroom where the bleach fumes were faint. The smell of males lingered on the clothes he'd sniffed. He could identify three of his pack who had been in Shannon's apartment. If she'd been there when they'd attacked...

He bit back a growl, furious over even considering what they could have done to her.

The odor of males who were *not* members of his pack worried him most. He caught the scent of at least two inside her room. Some of his pack obviously had started hanging out with unknown werewolves, came after a female behind his back, and disobeyed his orders. It would be unforgivable if he left and something happened to her.

"Let's go."

Her eyes widened and her pouty lips parted. "Go where?"

"My place," he instantly responded, not sure where else to have her stay. "I'm going to find the ones who did this and make sure they leave you alone before I allow you out of my sight." Inwardly he cursed, knowing it would lead to trouble. He currently resided in an apartment over a bar inhabited by his pack. "You can have the bed, I'll take the couch, and it won't take more than a day or two before you'll be safe on your own again." He hoped.

Shannon took a step back, tripped on a torn up pillow from her bed, and he lunged, grabbing her arm to keep her from falling on her ass. She hissed at him, a reminder that she wasn't completely human or any part wolf. He growled back instinctively and his hold tightened on her when he saw fear flash across her delicate features.

"Calm," he ordered her, wincing at the tone of his voice but unable to stop it. "Easy, kitten. I'm not going to hurt you and there's nothing to climb in here. Don't try to run from me."

Anger replaced fear as she glared up at him. "Stop calling me that! You just startled me. I'm not going to flee."

"Good. I'm the only thing standing between you and a bunch of wolves who have decided to play a game of fetch with you. They obviously mean business."

This can't be happening, Shannon thought, staring up at the mountain of a man inches from her. She inhaled his masculine scent and forced her racing heart to slow. *He's not going to hurt me.* She kept silently repeating that inside her head until her body relaxed. It wasn't the easiest thing to do. Instincts screamed at her to fight to get away from the big, deadly werewolf.

"I'm not going to stay with you."

"I'm not leaving you here alone. They *will* come back." Anton eased his hold but didn't release her.

"I haven't done anything wrong!"

"You are an enemy to werewolves."

"I'm not a shifter."

49

"I'm aware of that, but they don't seem to care *what* you are past how you smell and you're living on the edge of werewolf territory. The nearest pride is a good thirty miles from here. That means you're easy prey to my kind."

"Just tell them the truth about me."

"That won't help. That would just announce that you can't fight back. I purposely left out how human you truly are when I ordered the pack to leave you alone."

"You made a mistake. If you told them—"

"It wouldn't change a thing," he grumbled, releasing her and stepping away. "If they won't listen when I say you're off-limits, do you really believe they'll give a shit if you can't shift? I don't want to frighten you more but some of the wolves who did this aren't members of my pack. It means another pack is aware of you, or worse, they could be rogues. That means they answer to no one and don't live by any rules a pack has established. Do I need to spell out how much danger you're in?"

"I'll leave." Shannon blinked back more tears. "I guess moving a few blocks won't fix this. My mom lives in Ridley. I could go home to her." She dreaded doing that. Her mom had remarried to a man she couldn't stand. He gave her the creeps by leering at her sometimes and she always had to keep very aware of everything she did to avoid giving him any hints that she wasn't quite normal. "I have no choice."

"You're going home with *me*. No one would dare invade my den to go after you."

The blood drained from her face. "You literally live in the ground?"

"No." He shook his head, shot her a frustrated look, and his fingers rose to comb through his hair, pulling some of the thick strands free from the ponytail. "It's just a saying. It's an apartment over a bar. It's nice. Wolves don't usually live in actual dens. Wild ones prefer caves."

"That's good to know."

He shrugged. "Let's go, kitten."

"Stop calling me that."

He frowned at her again, took a step closer, and his eyes narrowed. "Let's get something straight right now. I'm in charge. I'm the one who will be protecting you because you need it. Stop arguing with me, it pisses me off, and just do what you're told. Otherwise, I'll have someone bring me a duffle bag, toss you in it, and take you out of here the way I would a cat with raised hackles."

Disbelief held Shannon silent for a few erratic heartbeats. "I didn't ask for your help and I don't want it. Leave my apartment."

He closed the distance between them and Shannon cried out in fear when he grabbed her. Her back hit the wall, bumping it painlessly. He pinned her between it and his big, powerful body. She stared into his angry gaze.

51

"Do you want me to tell you what those pups would have done to you if you'd been here when they came? You'd have been lucky if they just tore you apart with their teeth and claws while they killed you. They were male and you're attractive. I smell at least five of them total."

"No." Her voice shook, her body trembled, and horror spread through her at what he implied.

"Good." He blew out air, released her as quickly as he'd grabbed her, and backed up. "I'm going to make sure no one lays a hand, fang, or claw on you. Maybe I'll stop calling you 'kitten' when you stop acting so naive. I'm trying to do what I promised. Work with me."

"I don't know you," she stated honestly. "My instincts tell me not to trust you and I've been warned my entire life how dangerous shifters are."

He hesitated and something in his expression softened. "I always keep my word, and you're safe with me. I won't hurt you. I may growl and snarl a bit when I'm angry but I've never killed a woman in my life."

She swallowed the lump that formed in her throat. "I don't know what to do." It made her feel vulnerable to admit that.

His hand lifted slowly until his fingers lightly caressed her cheek. "I understand." He brushed her hair away from her cheek before he dropped his hand to his side, taking another step back, to put more space between them. "If it helps, I'm determined to keep you safe whether you allow me to or not. You can fight but you won't win. The decision isn't yours any longer. I couldn't look in a mirror again if I just stood by doing nothing while I knew you were in danger. My pups did this, and you've become my responsibility now."

Something clicked in Shannon's mind. "You've called them your pups before." Her tongue darted out to lick her dry lips. "Are you their alpha?" *Please say no,* she thought. Alphas were supposed to be the most brutal and ruthless werewolves of any pack.

He shook his head. "No."

The tension eased from her body and it gave her hope that he just happened to be a nice guy after all, albeit still a werewolf. His next words dashed that feeling as if he'd dumped cold water on her.

"I'm the son of their alpha, and I'm the first in line to take over the pack when he steps down or dies."

Her knees threatened to collapse but she fought the fear that surged as she locked her legs to remain standing. They watched each other silently for long moments before he glanced around her room.

"Let's go."

"My clothes—"

"Are all destroyed." He stopped at the door. "Stop wasting time. The faster I get you where I know I can leave you safely alone,

53

the quicker I can go handle this mess by tracking them down. I've got clothing you can borrow until we're able to buy you new stuff."

Shannon hesitated but then moved, stepping over the destroyed pillow in her path. She tried not to flinch as she took in the damage to her living room again. His pups were methodical in their destruction, not leaving anything untouched.

The apartment manager stood talking to the neighbors as they left. She opened her mouth to speak to the man but she never got the chance.

"I'm Anton Harris, a family friend of Shannon's." He directed an intimidating scowl at the manager. "I'm taking her to a safe location until they catch these punks. I expect you to have that door fixed immediately and guard her property until they are. I'm holding you personally responsible if anything else happens."

Her mouth dropped open and she intended to apologize but Anton chose that moment to reach back, grab hold of her limp hand, and gently lead her away from everyone. He walked her to the curb where a big black motorcycle was parked, released her, and climbed on the beast of a bike. He straddled the machine and arched an eyebrow at her.

"I know you can hold on tight." He leaned over a little, his hand reaching for something on the other side of the bike, and then he held out a helmet. "Close your mouth and climb on behind me."

Shannon considered refusing to leave with him. She could make a scene, and he wouldn't dare force her onto his bike with so many witnesses around. He'd flashed his license at the cop, giving away his identity. She stared into his eyes while he held out the helmet—and made a decision. He hadn't hurt her so far and someone definitely had it out for her, as her poor apartment, full of damaged possessions, could attest.

"Okay, but I'm holding you to your word."

"Good." He gave her a tight smile that didn't reach his eyes. "I'm the only chance you have of staying safe. You've got nothing to fear from me."

She didn't totally believe that but accepted the protective headgear and carefully put it on. It startled her as Anton reached up to secure the strap under her chin. Their gazes met and held until he finished.

"Ever ridden on a motorcycle before?"

"No."

Amusement flashed on his handsome, rugged features. "You'll enjoy it a hell of a lot. Just wrap around me, don't let go, and trust me."

Shannon hesitated. "The only person I could ever trust has been my mother."

He looked away, his gaze flickering anywhere but at her. "Sorry to hear it. Get on, kitten."

Irritation flashed at his nickname for her. She stepped off the curb and lifted a leg, awkwardly climbing onto the wide, long seat, grateful her loose skirt was easy to tuck firmly around her legs. It felt surprisingly comfortable to straddle the bike. Anton turned his head to peer at her over his shoulder while he lifted a second helmet.

"Stop calling me that."

"I told you why I do it."

"What the hell does that mean?"

He hesitated, tightening the strap under his chin, but never looking away from her while he did it. "I'm attracted to you, and I think you're cute. It would be flat-out stupid if I didn't remind myself of that every chance I feel my body respond to yours, considering that, by blood, we're sworn enemies."

His brutal honestly left her speechless. He winked and turned away. The motorcycle started, the loud engine stopping whatever conversation they could have had. She reached forward, hesitated, and then wrapped her arms around his waist. She had to press her body firmly against his broad back to lock her fingers together. She squeezed her eyes closed tightly and clung when he pulled away from the curb.

Chapter Four

Anton parked the bike inside the secure employee parking lot behind the bar. He killed the engine, grateful none of the staff stood outside the back door smoking. The arms around him loosened and the warmth snuggled against his back jerked away. He refrained from cursing when he realized he didn't like it one bit when Shannon separated their bodies.

He reached back, offering his hand. "Your legs may be sore so move slowly when you stand."

Irritation rose when she totally ignored his offer to steady her, avoided touching him, and climbed off the bike, careful not to flash him as she gripped her skirt. She took a few steps and then nearly fell on her ass after her legs buckled a little. He shook his head as he watched her sway before she caught her balance and turned to face him.

"I warned you. You said you've never ridden before."

"Did you have to hit every pothole and speed bump on your way here?" Her eyes flashed with anger.

Guilty, he thought, and hid the grin that threatened to curve his lips. "I have no idea what you're talking about," he lied. He'd never admit that he'd enjoyed her lush little body clutching him or how perverted he felt when he'd discovered that her hands lowered

57

precariously close to his erection when he'd had to drive over a speed bump on her residential street. It had taken hitting at least a dozen of them to put her hold where he'd wanted it—over his aching cock. It had been torture feeling her rub against him when the bike jostled them but he'd enjoyed every second of it.

"I swear, you gunned for every single one. I drive a lot and I've never had to go over so many of them."

He looked away before she could see his face, worried she'd guess he'd had ulterior motives. He braced a boot and stood, swung a leg over the seat, and refrained from adjusting his cock when the hard length pressed uncomfortably against his zipper.

"I took back alleys to avoid traffic." The lame excuse came easy. He held out his hand. "Take it. We're going inside and you're going to run into more of my pack."

Fear etched her delicate features and his protective instincts roared to life. It left Anton alarmed at his swift reactions to her emotions. He'd been raised to protect females but he admitted something was off. His response to her terror had his beast fighting to come out to defend her.

"Trust me."

He really wanted that from her, and worse, he needed it. He sensed it as vibrantly as he did the wolf living under his skin. He watched and waited for her to place her smaller hand in his. The tension rose between them until she stepped closer, looking undecided still, but then her palm brushed across his. His fingers wrapped firmly around hers and he tried to ignore how soft he found her skin.

"Do you want me to carry you? The last thing we need is you trying to climb the walls. I'd rather you just hang tight to me."

"No." Her chin lifted bravely and determination shone in her beautiful blue eyes. "I can do this."

He admired her courage but she'd admitted her control over her instincts wasn't the greatest. His hold on her tightened enough that he knew she couldn't jerk away from him. He headed toward the back entrance, silently hoping he'd be able to get her into his apartment without coming into contact with anyone.

Shannon tried hard to ignore the clawing terror that had her itching to run. She'd never had to face such strong instincts before and guessed the blame for it rested squarely on the broad shoulders of the sexy shifter who led her into his den. Her blood may have been diluted of shifter genes but fearing dogs, werewolves especially, seemed to be ingrained in her DNA.

The second he touched the handle of the door, she had to fight down pure panic that struck hard enough to make breathing impossible. Her hand tightened in his and he turned his head, giving her a concerned look.

"Are you okay?"

"What's *wrong* with me?"

He spun, released her hand, and an instant later she gasped when her feet left the ground and two strong arms came around her. Her back gently bumped the wall next to the door when he turned them, effectively pinning her with his body. He lifted her higher up on his chest until their eyes were level.

"Hold on to me," he ordered.

She didn't resist since her arms and legs wrapped around him faster than she could think. It helped, but not much. She stared wide-eyed at him and a soft growl came from deep within his throat. Shivers ran down her spine and a soft hiss escaped her parted lips. At the same time, she realized her fingernails bit into his shirt where her hands had slid under his jacket.

"Easy with the claws, kitten. I've got you, and what you're experiencing is normal. The scent of pack is very strong here. You may not realize you can smell it but you obviously can. You should see your eyes." He stared into them. "Damn."

Alarm gripped her. "My eyes? What's wrong?"

He studied the depths of her eyes and softly growled again. "Your body may not be able to shift but your eyes do slightly. You've got cat eyes now, bright blue ones with a hell of a lot of exotic yellow, and they are the prettiest things I've ever seen."

She glanced over his shoulder, gauged her vision for any changes, but didn't notice any. She looked back, staring into dark, intense werewolf eyes that seemed to have turned nearly black.

"Your eyes," she whispered.

"Yeah." He cleared his throat. "My voice is going to get deeper too."

She didn't need to be told that as she shivered again at his rough, slightly altered tone. "Why?"

"You're terrified but it's something else entirely for me."

"What?"

He softly growled again. "I want to fuck you so bad it hurts."

Mute, she gaped at him, never expecting him to say that to her. He closed his eyes and turned his head enough to expose his throat to her. She found her voice again.

"Are you offering foreplay? I remember what you said about sniffing your neck. I don't think—"

"If you brush your nose against my skin, I'll tear your clothes off and take you where we stand. I'm trying to get a grip on my wolf, and not looking at you helps."

"Put me down."

A louder snarl vibrated his chest against hers. "Don't fight me. You do and you're fucked in every sense."

She held very still, breathing softly, and watched his tight expression closely. His jaw clenched, flexing muscles along his jawline, and then his generous lips parted as he took deep breaths, which rubbed his chest against her breasts. To her shock, they responded, the nipples hardening, and a sound came out of her that she'd never heard before.

Anton's head snapped in her direction as his eyes flew open to stare at her with an intense, smoldering look. "You purr."

"I don't," she denied, despite the soft noise she'd emitted resembling exactly that.

"You—"

The back door next to them suddenly exploded outward when a tall woman barged from the interior of the bar, cursing a blue streak, interrupting whatever Anton had been about to say.

Shannon's eyes widened in stunned dismay when she realized the red stains on the white shirt and tight jeans the woman sported had to be fresh blood. It also marred the woman's hands.

"What happened, Glenda?" Anton snarled the words.

The woman spun, startled, and then bent, reaching for a hose attached to the side of the building. "Those stupid pups got in a fight while trying to play badasses for a few bitches. It's the beginning of when everyone starts going into heat but shit has already started for the pairing up." Her dark gaze shifted to Shannon and her eyebrows shot up. "Wow. Is that the bitch from up north? I thought she wouldn't arrive until tonight."

"Um..." Anton hesitated.

The muscled, at least six-foot-tall woman laughed. "What are they crossbreeding with up there? She's tiny. She part Chihuahua or something? It's insulting that a pack sent *that* for you to test out. They have to be desperate to hook up with a stronger breed. You're going to break her before the fun starts."

"Fuck," Anton grumbled. "Anyone dead inside?"

Glenda washed down her arms and hands with the hose to remove the blood. "Nope. We broke it up before it got that far. Von is making them pay for the shit they busted though. They took out five tables and dented a wall pretty bad but nothing a little drywall and paint won't fix."

Shannon gaped at the scary-looking woman. Thick muscles corded the woman's arms as she turned off the hose and straightened. Tattoos adorned both curves of her broad shoulders and peeked out from where her low-cut top dipped between her breasts. Shannon had no doubt that this was her first sighting of a female werewolf, and if they all looked like this one, they must be pretty darn vicious.

"Ban their asses. They know I don't tolerate that shit inside my bar."

"I already told them, Anton." Dark eyes lit on Shannon again and the woman moved closer. "Want me to get rid of that runt for you?" A cold smile formed on her lips. "Send a message that we're insulted at what they consider their best?"

63

Anton's body tensed. "Back off *now*, Glenda."

The woman froze and then made a strange face, her nose scrunching, and then a snarl tore from her parted lips. Pure rage transformed her features. "Puma! The fresh blood from the fight masked her scent at first."

If looks could kill, Shannon had no doubt she'd have died in that instant. The woman lunged forward, ignoring Anton's command.

He cursed and released Shannon with one arm, his open palm hitting the advancing woman hard in the chest. The push sent her staggering back and she landed on her ass.

"I said, *back off*," Anton roared.

A snarl came from the downed woman and she never took her hateful glare from Shannon. "Let me kill her! Please?"

Anton gripped Shannon with both hands again, his arms feeling similar to steel bands around her waist, and growled low and deep from his chest. "She's a guest here. You don't touch her. No one does."

Glenda turned her rage on Anton. "A *what?*"

"Guest. I've extended my protection to her."

The woman's mouth moved but no sound came out at first. Anger turned to amazement, then to confusion. "Why? She's a stinking *cat*. She probably came to play in our trash Dumpsters and you caught her. You have no stomach for hurting a female, even if it's one of those, do you? I'd be happy to take her ass out."

"I said she's under my protection—no one is going to harm her."

Glenda gingerly climbed to her feet, used both hands to brush off the backside of her jeans, and then gaped at Anton. "What the hell is up?"

He took a deep breath, his massive chest pressing tightly against Shannon's smaller one, pinned between his body and the wall. "Notice how faint her scent is? She's mostly human. Some of the pups decided to hunt her in the woods but I intercepted."

"She's the enemy. Of course they wanted to make her a chew toy."

"I don't allow aggression without provocation." Anton's features darkened with anger.

"She's breathing and has puma blood. That's enough provocation for me." Glenda shot Shannon a dirty look before meeting Anton's cool stare again. "I know you have a soft spot for women, so hand her over to me. I won't kill her but I'll at least dump her out of our territory."

"No."

Disbelief flashed on the female werewolf's face. "What are you going to do with her? Call her pride and have them meet up with you to return her?"

"No. She's going to stay inside my apartment until I make certain she will be safe in our territory. I'm giving her permission to stay. She lives on the outer edge and I'm granting her permission to stay there after I deal with the current threats against her."

A deep, vicious growl tore from Glenda before she spun away, marching toward the door. "I'm calling your father."

"Shit," Anton sighed, turning his head to stare at Shannon as the door slammed closed after the departing woman.

"You should just let me go stay with my mom."

Shannon studied his beautiful eyes. Her breath caught. He looked sexy to her, handsome. She noticed his strong, masculine scent, which she inhaled with each drag of air into her lungs, and her hands gripped him a little tighter. Heat flashed through her body until she squirmed, her thighs gripping his hips a little more firmly.

Anton softly growled and Shannon's breasts hardened at the vibrations it caused. The heat became scorching hot until she realized her breathing had turned into a borderline pant. They stared at each other for what seemed forever until he shifted his hips, snuggly resting the front of his jeans against her panties. Hard, aroused male rubbed against the core of her pleasure. A soft moan passed her lips, shocking Shannon.

"Damn," Anton rasped. "I'm too close to the heat, and I think you are too."

66

"You *are* really warm."

His gaze lowered to her breasts, smashed against his chest. "You don't know what I'm talking about, do you?"

"Your body temperature is hotter than normal and you have me pinned. Of course I'm hot. I'm going to start sweating if you don't put me down."

That hot, sexy gaze of his lifted. "Don't you go into heat? I'm talking about sex."

Stunned, Shannon swallowed hard. "No."

"You don't ache for sex sometimes more than other times?"

She shook her head. "No."

"Cats are different. You should go into sexual heat at least once a month if my intel is accurate."

"I am not going to talk about this with you." She blushed, embarrassed that he'd bring up something so personal. "But no, I don't."

"Werewolves have a time of year where we go into mating heat, and it starts in a few days. It usually lasts anywhere from about ten to fifteen days. It all depends on the year."

That stunned her. "I thought dogs were always horny." The moment the words were out of her mouth, she wished she could take them back, not wanting to offend him.

A grin spread across Anton's lips. "We are but this gets much worse. Nature's sick little joke on us to make sure we don't end up on the extinct list."

Questions flooded her brain but she didn't dare ask him. She bit her lip instead and lowered her gaze to stare at his tan neck. "I don't go into heat."

"I do, and that's why I'm going to drop you off inside my apartment now. You'll be safe if I leave you alone. The faster I can handle this mess, the better. You can't be here when mating heat starts."

He sighed, withdrawing the tight press of his hips from her. She refused to ask but she knew he had to have read her curious expression when he spoke.

"The urge to have sex is excruciating if you attempt to deny it. You don't want to be sleeping in my bed when it hits." He arched his eyebrows. "Understand what I'm hinting at?"

Oh yeah. Sweat broke out all over her body, imagining him super horny and determined to have sex with her. The idea didn't horrify her. The astonishment of that revelation cooled her down a little. *He's a scary werewolf, a full-on shifter, and in line to be a brutal alpha,* she reminded herself. *In other words, the last man I ever need to hook up with. It would be suicidal.* "You should put me down."

"I should but I'm not. I'm going to carry you into my apartment and then I'm going to go hunt down some of my pups. They're going to give me the names of their friends who broke into your apartment. Hopefully, by the end of the night, I'll have nipped this thing in the bud."

Anton ached to the point of pain from wanting to fuck the woman in his arms. He could take his pulse by the beat of it in his dick, throbbing painfully against his jeans. He pulled away from the wall, adjusted her weight, and fought a groan when her arms and legs tightened around his neck and hips. He knew what the term "like a second skin" meant now. Shannon would actually have to be a part of him if they were any closer.

He released her with one arm, jerked open the door, and stepped into the back area of the bar. The smell of his pack grew stronger, along with beer, and food. It helped drown out Shannon's arousing scent. He breathed deeply, walked quickly, and held her in a way that kept them from rubbing together too much. He took the back stairs two at a time up to his apartment. He paused, keyed in his alarm code, and the door popped open. He grinned, loving the new technology he'd installed recently.

He stepped through the open doorway and kicked it closed. He examined the small apartment with a quick glance, something he always did when he came home, and he sniffed the air.

"What are you doing?"

The soft voice made him smile at her pretty upturned face. Her eyes made him want to groan. They were exotic-shaped but the bright, brilliant blue with yellow flakes was a color he could get lost in. Fear made the yellow stand out more, nearly overtaking the blue. He found them entrancing.

"Making sure nobody trespassed while I was gone."

"You have a security system."

"I do but I can't be too careful. I have a lot of enemies as the son of an alpha." He cleared his throat. "Let go and I'll put you down. You're safe here."

He hated it when her arms and legs eased from around his body and he had to stop holding her. He liked the feel of her in his arms a little too much. She backed up the second her feet touched the floor and spun away from him to study his apartment with unabashed curiosity. He followed her gaze, hoping she didn't hate his bachelor pad. It looked a lot better now than when he'd taken it over from Grady.

"My brother lived here before me but he kept it pretty standard. I upgraded the kitchen and bathroom. I'm planning on putting up a wall to separate the bedroom area from the rest of it."

"It's nice. I actually love the open floor plan."

She had a great voice. Soft but a little husky. His dick throbbed harder. Mating heat couldn't arrive at a worse time. He could feel the need rising and his beast pressed hard against his skin, wanting to take the woman before him. It didn't care if she was the enemy. Her scent called to both sides of him.

"Help yourself to anything inside the fridge, and whatever you do, don't open that door. Nobody has the code to get inside but me."

She turned to face him and he took a step back. He fought the urge to lunge at her, pick her up, storm across the room to his four-poster bed and pin her under him. He glanced at her clothes, noting how easy it would be to tear them from her body to get them out of his way. He wanted to go skin to skin with her, rub his body over hers, and learn how she'd taste.

Fuck!

"Don't open the door. I have to go. Make yourself at home. Use anything you want."

He spun around, guessed she probably thought he had lost his mind or was just rude. He jerked open the door and slammed it behind him. He paused, touched the pad and locked her in. Better to be safe than sorry. He took a few deep breaths until her scent no longer tormented him and then forced himself to descend the stairs. He turned at the bottom and entered the business area of the building.

Noise and the scent of pack swamped his senses. He walked to the bar and nodded at Misty, the waitress behind the bar. She grinned as she approached him with a welcoming smile. The vibes

71

she put off when she locked gazes with him made Anton groan softly. He hated receiving green signals from women looking to attract his sexual interest.

"Hey, boss. You want something?" Misty leaned over the bar far enough to flash him cleavage.

"Knock it off," Glenda growled from his left. "He's not hooking up with you during the heat." She bumped his shoulder with hers. "What the hell are you doing?"

Anton sighed, turned his head and met her gaze, which was about level with his. "Nobody goes upstairs. I'm holding you personally responsible for her safety. You got me?"

"Yeah. I didn't call your dad."

"I didn't figure you would. You enjoy running the bar too much and you know I'd fire you in a heartbeat for being a tattletale."

"Who's upstairs?" Misty leaned over farther, revealing that she'd forgotten to wear a bra.

Glenda growled. "I don't want to see your tits and neither does Anton."

He glanced down the bartender's shirt and shook his head. "Not happening. I don't do employees."

"Damn. Then what do you want?" Misty straightened. "You're totally missing out."

"I have a dinner guest, so tell Ryan I'll be calling him in a bit to start cooking steaks for two. I'll be back in about three hours, so let him know to save a few if we run low. I want—"

"You've lost your mind," Glenda cut in. "You should let me get her out of our territory."

Anton growled at his longtime friend. "Stay out of this and do as I've ordered. Don't forget who's in charge around here. She's under my protection."

"The pack from up north already sent their offering? I thought she wouldn't arrive until after dark." Misty snorted. "I don't know why you even allow them to send their best women to make you sniff them. You'd never accept one for a mate."

Frustration filled Anton. "I don't need this crap now." He reached into his jeans pocket, yanked out his cell phone and scrolled through the numbers. He selected one and listened to the phone ring. His brother picked up after the fourth.

"I need a favor, Rave."

"What's up?"

"The Mortell Pack is sending this year's beauty queen for me to check out today. I want you to play me this time. I need you to cover."

"Oh hell no," his brother's deep voice rasped. "No way."

"You owe me." Anton paused. "I got you out of that mess last summer."

"Damn. Is she just really annoying or is she so hot you're afraid you'll end up mated to this one? Is it just for tonight?"

He hesitated and then sighed. "No. I want you to totally cover for me. I'll email you my schedule. I already have a woman who'll be in my bed."

"Anyone I know?"

"No, and it had better stay that way. She's off-limits. Will you do it?"

"Sure. I haven't hooked up with anyone yet. I'm free to fill in for you but you'll owe me for this one. There's mating heat, and then there's need-a-back-brace overindulgence. Women really try to impress the future alpha of a pack with vigorous...seduction."

"Thanks. Come down to the bar so you can head her off."

"I can be there in ten minutes."

Anton hung up and ignored the smirk Glenda directed his way. "I'm going out hunting. Protect her. No one—and I mean no one—goes near her."

"Fine." Glenda shrugged. "You're the boss."

Chapter Five

Nerves made Shannon's skin itch while she paced the small apartment. The scent of Anton lingered inside the room but became almost overpowering near his bed. She licked her lips and decided to take a shower. She could smell him on her clothes and skin. It had been hours since he'd left and she had no idea when he'd return.

The bathroom must have been recently upgraded because everything looked new. The only flaw in the design happened to be that there was no lock on the door. It made her leery of stripping naked but she longed to wash away Anton's scent from her body, hoping it would restore some sense of normalcy.

Hunger made her stomach rumble while she stood under the warm water pouring down her body. She'd skipped lunch and knew it had to be past her regular dinner hour. She'd always needed to eat more than other people, chalking it up to all the hyper energy that had plagued her throughout her life. She quickly washed her hair and then dried off.

She bit her lip, stared at her folded, dirty clothes, but avoided them. Shannon listened by placing an ear to the door until she became certain Anton hadn't returned. She eased it open slowly. All her senses seemed to have gone into hyperdrive since coming into contact with werewolves. It left her feeling disturbed, since she'd been so sure she hadn't inherited that many traits from her father. Now it made her wonder if those abilities had lain dormant as a result of never being needed.

The dresser contained nine drawers, which she stared at, wondering if anything he owned would actually fit her. It only took her seconds to decide she'd rather face the werewolf clothed than in a damp towel. She opened a drawer full of T-shirts, pulled out one, and dropped the towel. She tugged it on and it fell to mid-thigh. Anton happened to be really big and his shirt appeared as if it were a dress on her smaller frame. She opened another drawer, hunting for sweats.

"Shit," she gasped.

Her eyes widened in surprise at seeing the boxes. There had to be hundreds of condoms in every color and variation. She slammed the drawer closed to yank open another one. *Why does he need that many?* Her next thought gave her a sick feeling in the pit of her stomach. *How many women does he sleep with?* The mental image of Anton with other women left her feeling unsettled and decidedly bitchy.

The door beeped and Shannon spun around, straightened, and fear gripped her as she watched it swing open. Anton took a few steps into the room and then suddenly froze, his head jerking in her direction after he sniffed the air.

"I hope you don't mind but I took a shower and now I'm raiding your clothes."

She didn't miss the tense expression on his handsome features or the way his body seemed to stiffen until his hands fisted at his sides. His intense gaze lowered down her body and his eye color seemed to darken as she watched. He said nothing, didn't move, but seemed fixated on studying her bare legs.

"Did you find the men you were looking for? Is it safe for me to go home yet?"

He cleared his throat, refocusing his attention on her face. "No. It seems someone tipped them off that I was angry and they've gone into hiding. I'll find them. They have to show up for a mandatory pack meeting at breakfast and I'll be waiting for them when they do. I…" He lowered his gaze to her legs again. "I thought you might be hungry. I know I am."

"I'm starving."

"I'm having dinner brought up to us. It should arrive at any time. I called from my cell on my way back to let the cook know to prepare our meal."

"Thank you. Is there something wrong with my legs? You're staring."

He met her slightly amused look. "Sorry."

"Do you want to tell me where you keep your sweats?"

"You won't need them."

That raised her eyebrows. "I do. This shirt doesn't cover that much and I'll be more comfortable wearing something under it."

His nose flared and a soft growl escaped his parted lips. "You're not wearing panties?"

A blush warmed her cheeks. "I'm starting to realize that you have a bad habit of asking really personal questions. Which drawer do you keep your sweatpants in? I don't want to open any more of them, blindly searching for pants." She glanced at his condom drawer, then back at him. "I'm afraid of what else I'll find."

He grinned, obviously not embarrassed in the least. "All the other drawers contain clothing."

"I'm not even going to ask what you're thinking."

"Go ahead." He peeled off his jacket, blindly tossing it onto a chair by the still-open door. "What do you want to know?"

After a slight hesitation, she decided she might as well ask since it did make her curious. "Why do you have a lifetime supply of condoms? Is there something wrong with buying them a box at a time like everyone else does?"

"I told you, mating heat is approaching. I have no plans to take a mate and if I were to get a female pregnant, I'd be expected to commit to her. I'd rather have too many than not enough. I actually have more boxes of them stashed inside the bedside table."

Shannon knew her mouth dropped open as she gaped at him.

Anton chuckled. "What?"

"Those are some big boxes and that drawer is packed with them."

He took a step toward her. "And?"

"Do you really need that many?" The idea of having enough sex to use them all had her belly quivering, and his shirt suddenly seemed way too small.

"Mating heat is exactly the way it sounds." He took another step, closing the distance between them. "Think of it as going into a complete frenzy for sex."

"Oh." She wasn't sure how to respond to that.

Anton inched closer until he stood before her and she had to tip her head back to keep contact with his heated gaze. His hands unclenched and he reached for her. Shannon took a quick step back to avoid his touch but forgot the open drawer. The edge of it bumped against the back of her knee. She gasped from the sharp pain and would have lost her balance if Anton hadn't suddenly lunged to grab her hips. He yanked her against his body.

"Where are you going?" His voice deepened and he pulled her tightly against his larger frame. "You look as nervous as a kitten trapped inside a dog house." He grinned at his joke.

"That's not funny." She gripped his bare arms under his elbows and the second her fingers touched him, she gasped as a jolt of electric current seemed to spark.

"You look good wearing my shirt."

"Thank you." Shannon leaned back until her breasts weren't smashed against his chest, unsure of why he kept hold of her. "Do you want to let me go?"

"No." He paused. "You'd look better without it."

Her mind blanked, distracted by his touch and how close he stood to her. "Without what?"

"My shirt." His fingers tightened on her hips. "Why don't you take it off?"

"That's not going to happen."

"Why not?" Amusement flashed in his sexy eyes. He appeared flat-out heart-stoppingly handsome when his generous lips arched upward to create a naughty-looking grin. "I know I'd enjoy the view."

"I don't even know you and I don't have sex with strangers."

That drew a chuckle from him. "Who said anything about sex? Is that what you're thinking about?"

Shannon frowned in response. "You expect me to believe you wouldn't want sex if I were totally naked?"

"I'm a werewolf. We're comfortable with bare skin. If you'd been raised around shifters you wouldn't think twice about nudity around others. I admit, I'm very curious to see every inch of you." He slid his hands up to her waist where he gently squeezed. "You're soft here."

Her frown deepened. "Thanks for pointing out that I need to join a gym to lose the extra weight I've put on. I'm starting to see why you're still single. Here's a tip. It's not cool to point out belly fat or love handles on a woman."

"Most of us burn off calories faster than we can swallow them. Show me your body. I want to see this." He squeezed her again, fondling the soft contours of her hips and lower stomach. "Take the shirt off."

"I'm mostly human, remember? I'm not comfortable with being naked and I'm not stripping down to reveal the parts of me I normally wear baggy clothes to hide." She tried to step away but Anton held her firmly in place.

He suddenly released her and took a step back. Shannon relaxed, believing he'd decided to leave her alone. Her mind dismissed that assumption when she watched in stunned silence as Anton gripped his shirt, tugged it from the waistband of his jeans, and peeled it up his body.

The sight of his muscled, taut stomach and wide, impressive chest had her frozen where she stood, just watching as he tossed the discarded material to the floor. His grin widened and then he lifted one of his legs slightly, hooking the back of his boot heel with the front of the other one. He toed off both.

"What are you doing?" She found her voice and the ability to think again when his fingers gripped the front of his belt. She took a step back.

"What does it look like?" He worked the belt open and the sound of the zipper being lowered seemed unusually loud.

"Stop undressing!" Her gaze darted to the still-open doorway. "Anyone can walk in here."

"Is that the *only* reason you want me to stop?" He'd unsnapped the top of his jeans, allowing them to part into a vee that revealed he wore black underwear with a white elastic band adorned with a well-known designer name. "I thought you'd be more comfortable taking that shirt off you if we are on even ground."

There was no way she could ignore how in shape or appealing the big werewolf looked. Hands down, he had the best body she'd ever seen. Muscles gave him the sculpted appearance of a tanned, long-haired, breathing god. *A dangerous one.* A lump formed in her throat and she swallowed hard. *Stop gawking,* her mind ordered, but she couldn't tear her gaze away from his biceps when he rolled his shoulders as if he needed to stretch them a little.

"Is something wrong?"

"Um..." She finally regained control of her fascination with his muscles ripple and glared up at him. "No. Stop grinning at me. You're really enjoying making me uncomfortable, aren't you?"

His smile faded quickly and the amusement snuffed out of his dark eyes. "Is that what you are?"

She ignored his question, not sure of the answer. "What are you doing?"

"I'm trying to get to know you."

"By stripping?"

Anton flashed a grin again. "Can you think of a better way?"

"We could talk instead of showing off body parts."

Her gaze lowered to his chest and the urge to touch him suddenly arose. Instead, Shannon put more space between them, uncertain of why she longed to get closer to him. She took a deep breath and his scent slammed all of her senses. The wonderful masculine aroma coming from him drew a strange sound from deep within the back of her throat. Her nipples hardened and a rush of heat originated inside her stomach and quickly spread lower to create a definite throbbing ache at the core of her sex. The immediate and intense response stunned her.

"You're purring again." Anton's voice turned husky. "Aren't you curious to know what will happen if we get acquainted with each other a lot better, kitten?"

That question made her stop ogling his chest to shoot him a dirty look. "Curiosity killed the cat—and stop *calling* me that."

Anton's nose flared as he inhaled her scent. She couldn't miss the way his entire face tensed and a low growl emitted from him— before he lunged for her.

Shannon gasped as hands grabbed her hips again and his hot chest pressed tightly against hers. The way he smelled totally overwhelmed her when she sucked in a breath. She wanted to push him away but instead her nails bit into his skin where she clutched him, holding him there.

"Damn," He nuzzled the top of her head with his chin, forcing her face to push against him. "You smell incredible."

"I'm wet." She forced her hands to relax and then used her palms to push on his abs. "Let me go."

Anton's body pressed against her tighter instead of allowing her to put space between their bodies. "I can smell how aroused you are."

"I meant that I'm wet from the shower." Her heart raced and she trembled. "You—"

"You want me," he said, cutting her off, sliding his hands from her hips, his palms brushing the curve of her back before his fingers curled to firmly cup her ass. "As much as I want you."

Shannon gasped and pushed harder but she couldn't budge the wall of flesh trapping her tightly inside the cage of his arms. Her eyes squeezed closed while she fought back the moan that threatened to rise when he lowered his face to bury his nose against her throat. Hot breath tickled her and then his lips brushed the super-sensitive skin under her ear. His lips were soft at first, teasing, and then he nipped her suddenly, growling at her.

White-hot need flashed straight into her brain, making it impossible to think when her body burned for Anton. Her knees buckled but the man holding her didn't allow her to slide down his body. He kept her locked into place to nip her again, a little lower down the column of her throat, and the near pain of his teeth had her crying out.

"Anton?" a loud male voice interrupted. "Dinner is here."

The teeth gripping her skin eased and Anton released her with his mouth. "You have the worst timing, Yon." He set her on her feet and spun around, stepping between her and the door.

"Sorry, man." The guy sounded more amused than contrite.

Shannon reeled from the physical connection they'd just shared and her hand reached up to rub the wet spot on her neck. She stared at Anton's naked back, since he seemed to want to block her from whoever had brought their dinner. She lifted her gaze and saw red marks on the tops of his shoulders. She'd left them when she'd been holding on to him. Those half-moon shapes were from her fingernails digging in. He wasn't bleeding but they were definitely noticeable.

"Leave the tray by the door and go downstairs." Anton stayed close to her.

"So it's true that she's a cat-breed shifter." Something metal and heavy bumped with glass. "Misty has been spreading it around about how you're testing one out. I didn't believe it."

"Misty has a big mouth. You need to remind her to stop wagging her tongue, or I will."

The silence inside the room became absolute. Shannon leaned to the right and peered at a bodybuilder-sized blond guy standing just inside the apartment. He wore jeans and a red sweatshirt. He had his arms crossed over his chest, his eyes fixed on the floor, and his head dipped enough that his chin touched his chest.

"Understood," he said softly. "I'm sorry. She's my sister but she's young."

"I allowed her a job here but I don't need my private life spread throughout the pack. Damn it." Anton lifted a hand, finger-combing his black tresses. "If I catch hell for this I'm going to be pissed."

"I'm sorry," the blond muttered and then glanced up to reveal soft brown eyes. "I'll try to do damage control. I didn't think it would be a big deal."

"Have you met my parents?" Anton's hand dropped to his side. "I still have to answer to them."

"Your dad—"

"He's not the one I dread finding out." Anton glanced over his shoulder, met Shannon's gaze, and loudly sighed. "Trust me when I say we don't want my mother showing up to ask why you're here."

"You're afraid of your mommy?" Shannon couldn't help it. She grinned, finding it funny that someone his size and age feared his mother would disapprove of anything he did. "Will you get grounded for hanging out with me?"

"I'm out of here." The blond suddenly laughed. "Oh man, good luck with that one. I'll take care of Misty."

The door slammed closed, leaving them alone again. Anton's eyes narrowed dangerously and Shannon's grin faded. Obviously she had been the only one to appreciate her sense of humor. When he turned to face her, she backed up to put space between them.

"My mother is a bitch." He paused. "In every sense of the word. She's the alpha female and in charge of all the female members of the pack."

Shannon allowed his words to sink in, and with them came fear. "What would she do to me if she did come here?"

That drew a frown from him. "Nothing."

She didn't believe him. Something in his eyes belied what he said and she called him on it. "Seriously, don't bullshit me, Anton. Am I in danger from your mother?"

He hesitated just a moment too long. "My father wouldn't allow her to go after someone under my protection. I'll just have a talk with my dad if she discovers I'm harboring someone she considers our enemy."

"I really should go stay at my mom's place."

He closed the distance between them, his hands encircling her forearms. "No. I want you where I know you're safe."

"I'd be fine there." She didn't mention her stepfather or how she hated the way he looked at her as a sex object. She also worried about him figuring out there was something slightly different about her. For some strange reason she couldn't fathom, her mother loved the jerk, and she'd hate to cause problems within their relationship. "I'll get my paycheck and move to a new place. Besides that, I have a job I can't afford to get fired from, and that's exactly what will happen if I don't show up at work tomorrow."

"You'll call in sick until this is over, and I'm not letting you out of my den until I have a handle on my pack. I'll also find the males who aren't members of the pack and deal with them. You may not understand this but they know about you now. They will have declared a hunt."

"What does that mean?"

"It means they won't stop looking for you until they find you — or until I make sure they know I'll take out anyone who harms you."

Stunned, she gaped at him. "Take out?"

His eyes darkened to near black. "I'll kill them if they hurt you."

"You don't even know me. Why would you say something like that? I mean, you can't really—"

"You think like a human." He pulled her against his body, staring down at her with an intense look on his handsome face. "Your human world exists one way and shifter world is a whole other lifestyle. If you're under my protection and someone harms or kills you, it's not only my right but my duty to avenge you. Whoever dares violate my claim knows I'll come after them." His tongue darted out to wet his lips. "Is it so foreign to understand that I'd do whatever it takes to protect you?"

Shannon lifted her hands slowly, opening them on his chest. Her gaze lowered to stare at the hot skin under her palms. "Yes."

She felt the vibration of a soft growl. A flash of lust gripped her. For whatever reason, when he made those sounds, it seemed to excite her body into wanting him desperately. Heat from his skin penetrated the shirt she wore and she took a deep breath, pulling in that musky, masculine smell he carried. Her eyes closed and she leaned closer to brush her nose against his sternum. A soft noise came from her and it shocked her anew when she realized it did sound exactly like a purr.

Her eyes flew open and she jerked away.

"What is happening to me?" She flashed a frightened look at Anton.

One of his hands released her arm to tangle in her hair, cupping the back of her head. His face descended and his mouth covered hers before she could think. He didn't kiss so much as brand her with his lips, opening hers. His tongue invaded, tasting.

The only thing that existed was his mouth and the burning need to kiss him back. His other hand released her arm and wrapped around her waist, yanking her tighter against his large frame. Shannon clung to him as he lifted her higher, her feet left the floor, and on instinct she wrapped her legs around Anton. His open jeans fell lower until her inner thighs hugged his bared hips above the band of his briefs.

The sensation of his tongue melding with hers, rubbing and exploring, made thinking impossible for her until he dragged his mouth away. Both of them were breathing hard and as her eyes opened, she found herself nose to nose with him, staring into passion-filled, black eyes. The shape of them appeared slightly different, narrower and exotic.

"Don't fight it," he ordered, his voice deeper than she'd ever heard it.

He took a few steps and then bent, taking them both down onto his bed, pinning her under him. He used his elbows to brace his weight. Shannon realized the shirt she wore had ridden up to her waist when he pulled his arm out from under her to free it, his hand reaching between them.

With her legs still wrapped around his waist, her thighs were spread open to his seeking fingers, which zoomed straight to her sex. She was soaking wet with need as he spread her vaginal lips and rubbed her clit. Shannon threw her head back, crying out as pleasure swamped her.

"Just feel me."

Shannon bucked her hips when Anton massaged faster, strumming her clit. Her nails dug into his shoulders. Moans and purrs tore from her mouth as she struggled to get air. His hair tickled her neck and then his tongue licked her throat a second before he bit her. The sharp pain only rocketed the devastating ecstasy up another notch. Shannon gasped one more lungful of air and then screamed out when her world blew apart from the violent climax. Her body bucked but Anton held her down, forcing her to ride through it until he stopped touching her clit.

The sound of tearing material registered to Shannon but she had no idea what caused it. She also didn't care. Her vaginal walls shook and twitched from how hard she'd come. Each tremor made her gasp and the pleasure eased just slightly until something hard and thick brushed against the seam of her pussy.

Her eyes opened and she followed Anton's gaze down their bodies, where he concentrated with a tense expression on his handsome face. The front of his underwear had been destroyed, ripped open, and his heavy, thick cock nudged her pussy again, sliding in the slick heat of her release. A snarl came from Anton when he pressed against her a third time, but instead of entering, the bulbous tip of his thick shaft glided higher to rub her clit and ended up on her pelvic area.

"Fuck," he roared and suddenly pushed off her, and tore away from her body completely. He stumbled away from the bed.

Chapter Six

"What's wrong?" Shannon remained frozen where she lay sprawled on top of his bed, gawking at the totally naked man.

"I don't want to hurt you." The muscles in Anton's arms and even the ones cascading down his stomach stood out as though he'd been heavily exercising. "You're small and too tight."

She swallowed hard, her throat going dry. Her hands shook as she flattened them on the mattress, pushed up to a sitting position, and drew her knees closed. She huddled on his bed.

His lips parted, revealed some sharp-looking canines, and it struck her why his face suddenly appeared so frightening. He had started to shift a little into his wolf. It wasn't just the shape of his eyes that had slightly transformed but his lips looked fuller, his strong chin seemed to jut out a little more than normal, and those teeth weren't human. Her breath caught.

They watched each other and Anton stepped closer, then paused. His heated gaze ran over her body, lingered on her legs, and then he stood at the end of the bed.

"Take off that shirt and roll over."

Fear and uncertainty kept her frozen. Anton softly cursed and then leaned forward. His hands gripped her thighs and he flipped her over without warning. Shannon gasped, found her face pressed into his bedding, and then his hold changed when strong fingers curled around her hips. He jerked her up to her knees until her ass lifted high into the air, where he kept her suspended.

"When's the last time you had sex?" His tone turned rough, harsh.

It took Shannon a few seconds to be rid of her shirt and brace her hands. Clawing sheets, she pushed up to her hands and knees. She threw her hair out of the way by tossing her head and stared at him over her shoulder. She wiggled but his grip didn't ease, making it clear that he wasn't about to let her go. He put his knee on the bed, pressed against the back of her thighs, leaving her no choice but to spread them to make room for him.

"Answer me," he snarled.

"I..." She couldn't think when he climbed onto the bed, his body caging hers under him as he bent over her, his stomach pressing against her back. The position forced her to lower her head and chest closer to the mattress.

"We'll go slowly." He took a ragged breath. "Spread wider for me." He removed his leg from between her thighs and placed his knees on the outside of hers in a wide stance that gave her room to do as he demanded. "Now."

Their size difference frightened her. He had to have over a hundred pounds of weight to use against her if he chose and with his abnormal strength, she knew it would be a useless attempt to fight if she wanted to.

"Kitten," he rasped, his voice softening. "I smell fear and there's no reason for it."

Her mind started to work. He wasn't forcing the sex; in fact, he didn't try to enter her at all, waiting for her to move her knees apart. "You didn't get a condom."

The second the words were out, Shannon wished she could take them back. She should have mentioned her first concern—her fear that it would hurt since he happened to be the owner of one major hard-on. None of her previous lovers had come even close to being built as thickly as Anton.

"You're right." His eyes closed. "I'm not thinking clearly."

"We touch and that seems difficult to do for both of us." The fear eased from her body while she craned her neck to get a better view of his face.

He smiled, his tense features relaxed, and then he studied her. "I didn't mean to scare you."

"Your eyes have gone totally black. I can't see even a hint of brown anymore."

"It happens when I'm shifting."

"I'm not doing you as a wolf. That's just wrong on so many levels." She suddenly smiled, her sense of humor returning.

95

"Besides, your may get an uncontrollable urge to chase me or something since I'm part cat."

Shock blanked his features for an instant and then he laughed. "I wouldn't do that. I'm battling with my inner beast. We both want you pretty bad but I can hold my skin. It's just that when we're dueling for dominance, I can't hide what I am. My eyes darken, my teeth slide down, and it feels as if I've plugged my body into an electric current that makes every muscle tighten."

"Your bone structure slightly changes too."

"Really?" He reached up, explored his face with his fingertips, and then sighed. His hand dropped. "That doesn't normally happen. This is a mood killer, isn't it? I'm sorry. Let's eat before the food grows cold. I never meant to frighten you and I sure don't want to hurt you."

Shannon hesitated. "Get a condom."

"I think it's best if we calm down a little first. I need to get more control before I accidentally hurt you. As much as I want you, I always keep my word, even if I suffer blue balls as a result."

"I'm not afraid anymore."

"You should be." His gaze dropped to her ass and a soft growl tore from his throat. "You wouldn't say that if you knew how bad I wanted to fuck you. I'm going for sainthood at this moment. Trust me on that." His hand curving her hip flexed, gave her a gentle squeeze, before he pulled it away. "Let me get dressed."

He kept his back to her while he put on pants. Shannon hesitated and then climbed off the bed. Her hands trembled when she tugged on the discarded shirt. The dampness between her thighs a reminder that he'd gotten her off but he'd been denied that. She watched him fasten a pair of jeans, but he didn't bother with a shirt or shoes, and then he faced her.

"Let's eat."

Her gaze lowered to the front of his pants. The defined bulge displayed there was unmistakable.

"Don't look at me." His voice came out gruff. "I really want to get more control before we attempt that again. I would have been too rough with you. I know you're mostly human but my wolf doesn't seem to want to grasp that."

"I'm sorry."

"Don't be. I'm glad we stopped." He spun away and headed for the food. "I'd have felt like hell if I'd caused you any pain."

Shannon had to admit his response confused her. Most guys would be upset that the sex had come to a halt but he sounded almost relieved. She hugged her waist and watched him lift a large tray and carry it to the bar, then sit on a stool.

"Come on. We need to eat."

She forced her feet to move. Anton softly cursed, stood, and brought back two sodas from the fridge. She paused at the stool next to his and then sat. She glanced over at him.

"Why do you seem so relieved we stopped?"

He refused to look at her while he lifted one of the three plates off the tray to set it in front of her. "We shouldn't get involved sexually. It is a really bad idea, but when I touch you, I seem to forget that."

She inhaled the wonderful smells from her dinner. Someone had prepared a huge steak, some kind of stuffed baked potato, and a salad. She studied Anton's two plates, the same food she had.

"You eat that much?"

"Yeah. Werewolves eat a hell of a lot. I'll be ready for a midnight snack later. I take it you don't?" He finally fixed his attention on her.

"No. I'd be so big I wouldn't fit through doorjambs if I ate two dinners every night, and then ate again before bed. I've always struggled with my weight."

"You're very human, in other words."

"I guess so. I take it there aren't many overweight shifters?"

"There are some but it's tough to do. Our metabolism uses up calories quickly. Shifting burns a lot of them. If someone were to stay in one form for a long time they could manage to put on extra weight. I shift often."

Curiosity piqued, Shannon asked, "Doesn't it hurt? It looks painful. I always imagined it would be."

"It does at first but then you adjust." He picked up his fork and knife to dig into one of his meals. "How much do you really know about us?"

"Just what my father told my mother, and what she learned on her own as his wife. She always tried to remember everything to share with me."

"She's totally human?"

"Yes."

He looked at her. "And your father told her what he was? That's taboo."

"He couldn't really help it. He shifted in front of her. She said it scared the hell out of her. She ran but he chased her down."

"How did that happen? Didn't he smell her nearby before he shifted?"

She smiled. "Animal control had captured him with one of their traps. They injured him when it happened. He passed out and woke inside a veterinarian's office. My mother worked there. He came awake to hear the doctor say they planned to neuter him in an hour when they returned after lunch. Some zoo offered to take him if they neutered him first. He wanted to get out of there, as you can imagine, and needed someone to help him escape. He was smack-dab in the middle of a busy city area where they'd notice a naked guy or an animal his size. My mother just happened to be the one who walked into the back first. He shifted inside the cage, opened it and chased her. He borrowed a doctor's coat and forced her to drive him out of the city."

"She's lucky he didn't kill her."

"He thought she was the most beautiful thing he'd ever seen." Shannon smiled. "I heard that story from my mom a thousand times. My dad was really handsome, very sexy she said, and he fascinated her after her terror eased, when she realized he didn't plan to hurt her. She drove him to her grandfather's cabin, took a few days off, and patched him up. The trap had cut him pretty deeply. They fell in love."

"How did he die? We're extremely hard to kill, even mixed with human blood."

She met his curious gaze. "There was a fire. He got us out but an elderly woman lived in the apartment next door. He heard her calling for help." She pushed back tears and dropped her attention to her food. "He tried to save her, the roof collapsed, and they didn't make it out before it did. I can't remember much about him. Everything we owned burned. There aren't even any pictures to remind me of what he looked like. I know he loved us very much. It took my mom nearly ten years to even date other men. I think she only survived the heartbreak of his loss because of me."

"I'm sorry. He sounded real nice, Shannon."

He'd said her name. She turned to peer up at him. "He died a hero."

"Yeah, he did." He smiled. "Eat."

She focused on her food. The silence wasn't uncomfortable as they finished their dinner. He ate everything from both plates. He stood and cleared the counter, and then met her gaze when he came back to sit on his stool.

"You look like your mother, don't you?"

She nodded. "How did you know?"

He grinned. "You're the most beautiful thing I've ever seen. I can imagine how drawn he felt to her and how much he wanted to be with her."

A blush warmed her cheeks. "Thank you."

The distance between them suddenly disappeared when he leaned into her. He brushed back her hair. The light trace of his fingertips made her shiver with longing and passion flared in his sexy eyes. He growled softly, lowered his head, and breathed across her neck. His other arm wrapped around her waist to tug her against his body.

Desire shot through her and she knew she wouldn't resist him. She wanted Anton. The attraction between them too great to deny.

His lips caressed her skin under her ear and then he pulled back to study her.

His mouth opened but a knock interrupted whatever he'd planned to say. He muttered a curse, slid off the stool, and stalked to the door. Shannon hoped it wasn't his mother visiting. From what she'd heard about the woman, she guessed it wouldn't be a pleasant experience.

"What the—"

A tall, striking woman with jet-black hair in a single braid that fell to her ass shoved past a stunned Anton into the apartment. She wore all leather and resembled something out of a sexy action film, with the way the outfit formed tightly against her body. Green eyes actually flashed at Anton. Her hands gripped her hips and one of the spike heels of her black leather boots tapped the floor. Her chest pushed forward and her skintight top parted slightly to reveal the generous curves of tanned breasts.

"You insult me, Anton Harris. You sent your younger brother to meet me. I will not settle for some pup! You will not slight the Mortell pack this way."

Anton gaped at the woman.

She turned her head, spotted Shannon, and sniffed. Her features paled suddenly and then a snarl tore from her mouth. Her fangs literally grew longer, her nose wrinkled, and she lunged toward Shannon.

"No!" Anton leapt into the woman's path, his arms spread wide to block her and keep her back.

Fear stabbed hotly at Shannon and she turned, instincts taking hold, and leapt on top of the counter. She ran along it until she hit the wall. She spun, trapped there, and desperately searched for an escape route. Her gaze fixed on the window not too far away. They were on the second floor of the building. She still wanted to fling her body through the glass, even knowing it might kill her.

A terrifying snarl sounded again to draw Shannon's attention. The woman had crouched down, one hand balanced on the floor, which now had long claws instead of fingernails, and her features had shifted enough that a black spread of hair covered her cheeks. Her jaw had elongated into more of a muzzle than a mouth, and very sharp-looking white fangs were revealed more clearly. The woman's green eyes had narrowed, shifted shape, and the sound had come from her.

"Move out of my way." The woman's voice sounded more masculine than feminine.

"No," Anton snarled back, his voice equally as terrifying. "She's under my protection."

Someone pounded up the stairs and then a muscular, burly guy with long hair barreled into the room. He nearly tripped over the half-shifted werewolf woman prepared to attack but drew to a jerky stop just in time to avoid a collision. The new guy looked very similar to Anton with his long black hair, jeans, and a tank top that revealed tattoos spread across broad, muscular arms. Shannon guessed they had to be brothers.

"I tried to stop her," he panted. "She didn't take meeting me well, knocked me on my ass, and she can move swiftly when pissed. It seems she somehow knows what we look like."

"Get her out of here, Rave," Anton snarled. "I don't care how." His gaze remained locked on the woman threatening Shannon. "If she tries to get around me it's going to cause a war between our packs, because I'll throw her out myself. She won't enjoy flying out a window or down the stairs."

Rave suddenly stopped breathing and his head turned. His dark gaze sought and found Shannon. Confusion reflected on his features and then his eyes widened with shock. He sniffed loudly. "Puma? Seriously? Oh, shit."

He didn't snarl at her or growl. Shannon figured that had to be a plus. He glanced away from her to frown at Anton.

"Why do you have her here?"

"She's under my protection." Anton snarled again at the woman on the floor. "Do you understand? You attack her and I attack *you*. You will never reach her."

The woman slowly rose up, her terrifying features still in a half-shifted state, and she defiantly stared at Anton. "You *dare* insult my pack by preferring to fuck one of them over me?"

"Fuck?" Rave gasped. "Who said anything about that? He said he was protecting her for some reason."

"I smell them," the woman spat. "Sex and desire."

Rave sniffed again. He blinked a few times, his gaze passed from Shannon to Anton, and he suddenly laughed. "Oh shit. This is...wow!"

Anton glanced at her. "Don't move, Shannon. I'm coming to get you." He shot a warning look at his brother. "Don't let that bitch attack. I need to get to Shannon. She's too close to the window. She can't control her fear."

Rave hesitated and then stepped around the angry werewolf woman to put his body between Anton and her. "Do you want to tell me what the hell is going on here? Deana, I suggest you calm down. I know you're not happy over meeting with me instead of my brother but you can't attack someone under his protection."

"She's a puma." Deana snarled again, growled, and her fingers lifted to display her sharp claws. "They are our enemy."

Anton spun toward Shannon and he eased forward. "Easy, kitten. You're safe. Don't move, okay? You're in no danger."

Fear nearly overpowered her as she glanced at the window again. A soft sound escaped her lips—a whimper. Anton softly cursed in response.

"Shannon? Look at me."

She did. She took a deep breath, trying to fight the urge to jump away from him. He wouldn't hurt her, she knew that, yet another snarl from the werewolf bitch had her turning toward the window. The urge became so powerful that her body tensed in anticipation of jumping to reach it.

Anton surged forward. She hissed when he grabbed hold of her ankle. He jerked hard and she tumbled off the counter. She landed inside the cradle of his strong arms when he caught her. Shannon turned against his chest and clawed at him. He groaned but then pressed her against the wall.

"Easy," he crooned. "I've got you. Hold on to me."

She panted, fought her instincts, and realized what her fingernails were doing. She jerked them away from his skin. The smell of blood filled her nose and she saw she'd drawn it from him. She'd marked his flesh, her nails had pierced him.

She wrapped her arms around his neck to hug him tightly. Hot tears spilled from her eyes.

"I'm sorry."

"I'll heal. It's nothing. It won't even leave a scar." He nuzzled the side of her face. "I'm just happy you don't have claws."

His hold on her changed enough that she could wrap her legs around his hips. It made her feel better to totally press against him. "I'm sorry," she sniffed again. "I didn't mean to do that."

"Shush. It's okay." He turned his head. "Get that bitch out of here, Rave. *Now*. Handle it."

"I won't leave." Deana's voice still sounded masculine. "*She* will. If you insult my pack this way, I'll make sure my father demands retribution."

Anton turned, holding Shannon. "I don't want you. It's not personal. You're beautiful, Deana. That's your name? Any male who wasn't involved with a woman would be lucky to have the opportunity to test a mating with you, but as you can see, I already have someone."

"She's a cat shifter." Deana spat the words as if they were a great insult. "That's sick!"

"She's mostly human. That's why the scent of her is so faint that you didn't detect it immediately. She can't shift. She's no an enemy of mine." He paused. "She matters a lot to me. I'm sorry that you aren't happy with being offered my younger brother, but Rave isn't attached to anyone. He's a strong male, a prime mate candidate, and he's the main enforcer of our pack. You won't find a better fighter. He may appear mellow but you've never seen him enraged."

Shannon felt safe enough to turn her head to watch the terrifying female werewolf. Deana's features had shifted back but her fangs still dented her human-looking mouth.

"You're the future alpha of this pack. I'm the strongest daughter of the Mortell pack. We would be a good match. I could be your alpha bitch and help you hold your pack when you take control." She shot a hateful sneer at Shannon. "*That* is dinner."

Shannon trembled from fear. She wondered if the woman meant that literally. *Do shifters eat each other if they're from different races?*

Anton's arms tightened around her and he nuzzled her cheek with his jaw to comfort her. "She's under my protection and you

107

will *not* insult her. This is my home. I've offered you the best candidate our pack has to offer who's available to test a mating with you. Deal with that. I'm taken."

"Shit," Rave rasped. "Does Mom know? Dad?"

"Shut up," Anton demanded.

"Damn. Okay. That's what I figured." Rave met Shannon's gaze and gave her a tense smile. "Nice to meet you."

Her mouth parted but no words came out.

Anton sighed. "She's terrified. She can't shift but her instincts are present. Obviously. You saw how fast she can move when fear grips her. Terror makes her climb and try to get away from whatever scares her."

"That's why she's wrapped around you like a second skin." Rave laughed. "I guess dating her means you're going to get laid a lot. You terrify everyone, and with her constantly wrapped around your waist, she won't be able to get away from you every time you raise your voice. That's really convenient."

"Damn it, Rave. Stop with the jokes. Does this seem the time for them?"

"Probably not, but damn, bro, you've got to admit that this is priceless." He chuckled. "She's really cute. Her hair is beautiful and her eyes are amazing."

"I won't be insulted this way!" Deana huffed. "I'm calling my father." She spun and stormed out of the apartment. Her high-heeled boots struck loudly on the stairs as she retreated.

"Fuck," Rave sighed, all traces of humor gone. "You know what that means. She's going to call her daddy, who will in turn call to chew out our dad's ass. If our parents didn't know about your sexy little cat before, they will real soon. I wouldn't want to be you."

Anton growled. "Great. It's Mom I'm worried about."

"Oh man." Rave shivered. "She'll come here to verify if it's true." He pulled out his keys. "Take her to my cabin if you need a place to hide out." He removed a key and tossed it.

Anton released Shannon to catch the key then his arm wrapped back around her with it fisted in his palm. "Thanks, but I won't need it. This is my home."

"It may be but sometimes it's better to run than fight. Braden was there last so I'm not sure what condition he left it in, but I'd take food. That kid can eat."

"I refuse to hide out as if I've done something wrong that I'll be grounded over. I'm an adult. I'll deal with our parents."

"Better to have a backup plan in case you need one. That's my life motto. I can't say I'm upset that bitch just rejected me. Did you see that leather outfit?" He shuddered. "I wouldn't be surprised if she owns whips and chains, her idea of a fun, sexy time being to draw blood and attempt to restrain me to a bed. Not my thing. The only one getting tied down in my bed are women who like to wiggle around too much while I'm eating them."

Shock widened Shannon's gaze as she stared at Anton's brother. He glanced at her and grinned.

"I'm talking oral sex, kitten." He chuckled. "That's a cute name for her. Appropriate."

"Don't call her that. She doesn't like it."

"*You* called her that."

Anton softly growled. "Rave, it's time for you to leave."

"Do you want me to hold her while you try to talk that bitch out of calling to tell her daddy about you? It may be a good idea. You could avoid a lot of hell if our parents don't find out you're harboring someone they'll consider an enemy."

"No." Anton took a step back. "You aren't touching her."

"I wouldn't hurt her. I seriously mean it." Rave's features hardened, all humor disappearing. "I won't hit on her either. My tongue will stay inside my mouth and my zipper will remain up. You might consider going after that bitch to stop her. Our parents aren't going to be happy that you've got her here. I don't know what will be worse—that she's part puma or that she's mostly human. You're the future alpha of the pack and they're going to pitch a fit, worry that you'll decide to keep her past mating heat. That's a serious commitment to make, having her in your bed for

110

the next few weeks. It's one thing to experiment with a one-night stand but you've obviously chosen her to share the heat with."

"I haven't," Anton denied. "A few of our pups discovered her and kidnapped her to hunt in the woods. I drove her home after saving her from them. I thought she'd be safe but they visited her apartment and tore it up. I brought her here to protect her until I can rid her of the threat."

"It's too close to mating heat." Rave crossed his arms over his chest. "If it hits with her here, you're going to take her, and once it starts you know how it is. She's in your home. This isn't running into the woods to nail any female offering it up for a free-for-all. You're attaching her scent to you too strongly for your wolf to want any other bitch. Or I guess I should say she-cat, in her case. You won't be able to get enough of her and if you try to fight the urge, it could turn ugly. Denying what your animal demands in mating heat tends to cause accidental mating. Just ask Grady about that. He tried to deny his wolf with Mika, and he lost control until he claimed her permanently. It worked out for them, but he passed on being alpha. You don't have that option."

"Don't worry about it."

"They'd never allow her to hold the position of alpha bitch, Anton. She's part *puma*. Mom would go insane, and I can't see our father taking it well either. Then there's the reaction from our entire pack to consider."

111

"Damn it," Anton snarled. "Just go. I'm protecting her, nothing more."

Rave sniffed. "Is that what I smell? Your version of guarding her body? The lust is strong in here."

"Just leave." Anton spun around, moved toward the kitchen and sighed. "Please close the door on your way out."

"Use the cabin if shit hits the fan. Good luck, Bro. You know I love you and support you regardless of pack politics. I always have your back."

Anton halted but he didn't glance at this brother. "Thanks. I love you too."

"You make a cute couple." The door slammed closed.

Shannon peered up at Anton. He looked angry when he met her gaze. "It will be fine. There's nothing my parents can do to you. You're totally safe."

She really doubted it. "You should really just let me go stay with my mom."

He shook his head. "It's not happening."

Chapter Seven

"Who was that woman?" Shannon allowed Anton to set her on top of the counter.

He released her, stepped back, and frowned. "Mating heat is about to start. Other packs wish to unite with ours. Different ones send women here to see if I'll hit it off with them."

Shannon silently gawked at him. She finally found her voice. "As in you take her to dinner and get to know her? She wasn't exactly dressed...well, to go out anywhere unless it's to a strip bar. That outfit left little to the imagination. I can't believe she goes out in public."

His dark head turned away and she could have sworn she saw him blush. "Not exactly." He glanced back at her and crossed his arms over his chest.

It sank in slowly. "Oh my. You're supposed to have sex with them?"

"Yeah."

Emotions flooded forth, mostly jealousy. The idea of Anton with other women just didn't sit well with her. The scary beauty queen the other pack had sent made her feel worse. That woman possessed a porn-star body in her skin-tight leather jumpsuit. She'd been about as different in appearances from Shannon as she could get. It also became clear that the guy had probably slept with a lot of women in his lifetime.

"Every year, you have to sleep with one woman to see if she's a possible mate?"

He glanced away again. "Not just one."

She knew the color drained from her face. "How many women are you supposed to sleep with during this heat thing?"

"There are a lot of packs out there who would love it if one of their daughters mated with the future alpha of our pack. We're stronger than most and have prime territory. I get sent one every day from the different packs during mating heat. They schedule the days with my father."

"How long did you say this thing lasts?"

"Anywhere from ten to fifteen days. It depends on the year. It's difficult to predict. Sex is an effective way to test if we're mates."

Her shock turned to a sick twist in her stomach. "I'm leaving."

She shoved off the counter, landed on her feet, and walked for the door.

Anton moved faster than she could, his body blocking the only exit, and he frowned down at her when she halted. "It's not safe for you to go."

Embarrassment and humiliation surfaced. She refused to look into his eyes, instead focused on the mouth that had been on her body recently. She'd thought they might have had something

114

unique, perhaps the beginning of something real, but instead he just had sex with a lot of women. He had to be one serious player to take sex that casually.

And she'd almost allowed him to fuck her. She would have if he hadn't halted it.

"Get out of my way, Anton. I'm out of here. No wonder you have so many condoms stashed."

He sniffed and softly cursed. "Damn."

"I'm not turned on." She backed up to put space between them, spun around, and her gaze lifted to the window she'd contemplated leaping through earlier. It looked tempting again. She just needed to get away from him. She'd totally made a fool of herself by allowing him to touch her. "I just need to leave before the next one arrives."

"I know exactly what you're feeling. You're hurt. I can smell it."

She refused to look at him. "No, I'm not," she lied, unwilling to allow him to know she'd started to grow too attached to him. "Get your nose checked. I just don't want to be here when another werewolf woman arrives and threatens to make me her dinner." She tried to nonchalantly inch closer to the window. "You're too busy with your schedule to babysit me."

"Damn it, Shannon. Look at me." He growled the order.

She turned her head. "What?" Her gaze met his and regret simmered in his brown eyes.

"It's not what you think."

"What am I thinking?"

"Hell." He blew out air. "I don't invite them."

"But you've sure slept with a bunch of them. Wow. You poor baby. You've got such a sad life. All those werewolf women showing up every day to have sex with you must be traumatic. You said your father schedules them to see you, right? That implies he has your permission. Is there a sympathy card I can send you for that?"

"This isn't— Shit, I don't even know what to say." He lifted a hand to run his fingers through his hair. He tore out the ponytail holder and tossed it aside, shook out his long tresses until they fell around his shoulders and grimly studied her. "I know it sounds bad but I wish you'd at least let me explain."

"What's to explain? I was here when no one else was, so you thought you'd amuse yourself with me regardless of the fact that you had to realize I don't just mess around with guys for fun. You knew I wasn't that type." She put a few more feet between them. "Maybe I'm a novelty to you. Ever done a part-puma shifter before?" She jerked her head toward his bed. "Are there hidden notches somewhere over there that I missed seeing? I *am* short. Maybe you keep them high on the posts."

He snarled. "You're making it sound..." He closed his mouth and shot her a glare.

"Dirty? I guess that's exactly what it was. I've never been so happy not to have gone all the way with a guy. Are you going to let me out of here?"

"No. You're not safe out there alone."

"Nothing I say will change your mind about allowing me to leave?"

"Hell no. Not until I know no one poses a danger to you."

"That's what I thought." Her body tensed as she took a deep breath. "I'd rather take my chances out there than be used by you. At least whoever comes after me will be honest about wanting to cause me harm."

She allowed her instincts to take over, encouraged them, and suddenly sprinted toward the window.

The rumor that cats really did land on their feet giving her the hope that she wouldn't get hurt. She jumped, her arms lifting to protect her face and throat, but she never hit the glass.

Two strong arms grabbed her instead and they slammed into the wall inches away from it.

"Are you insane?" Anton raged.

She would have told him no but she couldn't breathe. He'd nearly crushed her when they hit. His large body pinned hers in place and then he leaned back. She drew in a deep breath and started to struggle.

"Let me go!"

He refused, instead holding her tighter, and walked toward the bed. He tossed her so she landed in the middle of it. She scrambled to sit up and then rolled off the other side to keep the large mattress between them.

"I want to leave." She glared at him. "If you won't allow me to walk out the door, I'm willing to test a theory by going out the window. The only danger I'm in comes from the next woman who gets mad that you've sent your brother to meet her in your place."

Anton snarled, his eyes darkening to black. "You're taking this all wrong."

"What have I misunderstood? You have sex with a lot of different women, it doesn't mean anything to you, and I am *not like them!*"

"I didn't say you were. You have no idea what my life has been like. Since I could walk, my father has been grooming me to take over the pack one day. I have a shitload of responsibilities and taking a mate is one of them. There are pack rules to follow and obligations to be met."

"Then I've never been happier in my life to have avoided all shifters and be on my own."

"I didn't touch you because of boredom. I'm genuinely attracted to you, Shannon."

"Excuse me for not finding that noteworthy. It sounds as if my having a pulse is all it takes for you to feel drawn to me."

"You're purposely trying to anger and insult me."

"That would imply it's possible to do that. Obviously you don't have many standards if you allow your father to rule your sex life. Have I said anything that isn't true?"

He growled, flashed his fangs at her, and took a threatening step forward.

She hissed at him. She hadn't meant to but the sound still pushed past her parted lips. She lifted her hands, fingers curved, implying she'd scratch him if he tried to touch her. He paused.

"Stay away from me. I mean it. Go after that bitch if you need to nail someone. I sure as hell won't allow you to touch *me*, now that I know your dance card is full."

"Damn it!" He took a step back. "You're really hurting. I can smell your pain. You don't mean what you're saying; you're just trying to wound me with your insults. We're attracted to each other. I realize you don't allow many males near you."

"I'm totally not your type—and you aren't mine. I should leave now. I'll be fine with my mother. Give me a cell phone number to reach you at and I'll call within a few days. You can tell me when it's safe to leave her house."

"I don't want you to go."

"I'm not staying."

She glanced at the bed, the one she'd been on so recently, allowing him to do things to her, and she wrapped her arms around her waist. The memory of it made her want to cry. She'd foolishly allowed him to get beyond her defenses, his touch going deeper than just her skin, and she'd started to fall for him.

"I need to leave." She met his gaze. "I heard what your brother said. No way am I sticking around, risking you going into heat. I won't allow you to ever touch me again."

"It's not... Shit. You're not listening to me. It wasn't just sex, Shannon. I want you to believe me. It's the truth. My oldest brother, Grady, warned me that allowing my father to schedule meetings with prospective mates would bite me in the ass one day. I guess it's today."

Shannon watched him. She'd thought he looked handsome, still did, but now she knew what kind of life he led. He had sex with a bunch of different women, often. She'd always avoided one-night stands or allowing a guy to touch her too quickly in order to escape these painful situations. She'd bypassed her own rules because she'd just been too attracted to Anton Harris. She'd thought there was something special between them, something meaningful, but it had only been on her part.

A horrible thought struck. "Oh no. Tell me you've been tested. If you've slept with a lot of women, your chances of an STD are higher than normal."

"Shifters don't carry sexual diseases."

"Good." Her shoulders slumped. "I guess that's one bright side to this, but it seems everyone you know wants to either kill me or make me their dinner. You keep telling me I'm in danger but you seem to put me in more of it than I'd find on my own."

"You're under my protection."

"Then just announce that and allow me to walk out the door."

"I need to guard you."

"That's bullshit. If I go to my mother's, they won't find me there. I won't go to work until this is over. They tore up my apartment and my uniforms and paycheck stubs were there, so they'll know where I work. But they wouldn't have figured out where my mom lives."

"They may have found her address in your apartment."

"We see each other enough that we don't send mail back and forth. I never wrote down her address. I just drive there. She's remarried, everything is under her new husband's name, and I'll be safe."

Anton shook his head. "I won't allow you to leave me."

She stared at him silently. She didn't understand his persistence to keep her with him. It didn't make any sense. He should *want* her gone so he could sleep with lots of other women if he enjoyed that kind of lifestyle. It was unsettling how much he confused her.

"I won't touch you again, okay? I'll be on my best behavior. That should alleviate the conclusion that I only want you for sex."

121

She studied him. "What about when the next woman arrives for her appointment with you? Is she going to try to attack me too?"

His jaw clenched. "Rave has taken over those duties for me until I've established that you're safe from the males hunting you."

"And if you go into heat? Then what?"

He glanced away. "I've got a few days."

"Look at me."

He met her gaze.

"What happens if you go into heat and I'm still here in your apartment? Tell me the truth."

His licked his lips. "You're fucked, kitten. Often. By me." He dropped his arms to his sides where they fisted. "In the literal sense."

"You said it's hard to predict this mating heat thing. What if you're wrong and it starts tomorrow? Or worse, tonight?"

He hesitated. "Would it really be so bad?"

"Yes," she stated clearly. "I am not the casual type, Anton. You said you smelled my pain. I can't get involved with you. I'm grateful for all you've done, I owe my life to you, but I'm not willing to get my heart broken if something happens between us. You'll go on your merry way to someone else and I'll really get hurt."

He growled and then spun away. He put on a shirt, his boots, and a belt. He never looked at her while he dressed and stomped to the door. "I'll go hunt down those males and deal with this now. Don't try to leave, Shannon. You don't want me hunting you. Trust me on that. If you do..." He stopped at the door and turned his head to glare at her over his shoulder. "I'll finish what we started, only I'll be too pissed to care if I harm you because my wolf will be in charge. You wouldn't like me out of control. I gave you my word that no harm would come to you, and I will protect you — even if it's from me. I'll be back soon."

He slammed the door behind him. She heard something beep and ran for the door. She tried to open it but it refused to unlock. He'd managed to trap her inside his apartment.

Her gaze darted to the window. It would be her last option to get out.

"Shit!"

* * * * *

Fury drove Anton to kick in a door to the house where several of the pups lived together. Three of them sat on a couch playing video games. He snarled when he met their shocked gazes.

"Where are they hiding?"

A blond teenager paled. "They didn't say."

Anton didn't have to mention names. He studied Kyle, the blond, and showed his fangs. "What do you know?"

"They decided to go after some cat, and I know that's why you're here." He glanced nervously at his roommates. "They hang with some rogues who thought it would be fun to go after her."

"Shit," one of the younger males cursed. "I didn't know." He gave Anton a terrified look. "I swear. I would have reported it if I'd known anyone hung with rogues."

Anton walked to Kyle, leaned over the frightened teen, and snarled, "Where do they meet? They must have somewhere they hang out together to avoid being seen by anyone in this area."

"In the woods, at the north end, but I swear that's all I know! I told them not to piss you off. I warned them what would happen if they didn't obey your orders. I didn't do anything to that puma shifter. You made it clear how angry you were and you said to leave her alone."

Anton glared at the three. "Go hunt them down and bring them back here. I want the rogues too. Call me on my cell when you have them."

The three nodded eagerly and bolted for the door. Anton left the house, still longing to beat on someone, but knowing he had to attempt to calm down. It wasn't so much that the pups had disobeyed him or that they were hanging out with undesirables that angered him. Pups did those things, needed to learn to obey orders, and it had just become part of his job to deal with them. It wasn't anything new.

What irritated him the most, made him killing mad, had been Shannon's reaction to learning about his life.

My having a pulse is all it takes for you to feel drawn to a me.

He couldn't get Shannon's accusation out of his head. Her words repeated over and over. He growled low under his breath. The sad thing, he admitted, was that it wasn't that far off the mark. He had allowed a parade of bitches to stroll through his life, to fulfill his duty to find a mate who would help lead the pack when he had to take over the alpha position.

The scent of Shannon's pain and the look of betrayal in her beautiful eyes haunted him. He hadn't wanted to lie to her when she'd asked her questions but his answers had struck her as if he'd backhanded her across the face. She'd closed down on him. Hell, she had tried to leap out a second-floor window just to get away from him. Their touching had been incredible but now she thought it amounted to something meaningless and dirty. She'd asked about sexually transmitted diseases!

He snarled, straddled his motorcycle, and fought the urge to throw back his head to howl in rage. He wanted Shannon unlike any other woman he'd ever known. It didn't make sense. He knew it couldn't work out with their bloodlines but he didn't care about logic or odds. Neither did his wolf. He ached to touch the mostly human shifter to the point of pain.

I should have taken her when I had the chance. Now she would never allow him to touch her again. *Not unless she's really scared and wraps around me.*

A slow smile spread across his face. It would be underhanded and wrong, but he wanted her that bad.

"Fuck." He tore down the street on his bike to return home. "I can't do that to her. I'm not an animal. At least not totally," he muttered.

He parked behind the building and entered the back door. The noise from the bar drew him inside. The room nearly overflowed with shifters from his pack and visiting ones. He scanned faces, couldn't recognize about forty percent of them, and then located Glenda. She'd exchanged her bloodied white shirt for a blue tank top and black snug jeans.

Males studied his friend but few approached her. She intimidated most werewolves. She stopped at a table to talk to a few bitches, not from their pack, and then spun toward the bar. She appeared angry when their gazes met. She changed direction and headed his way instead.

"You've got fans. They want to meet the Harris boys." She rolled her eyes. "I told them to pair up with someone else. Pathetic groupies. They don't even have alpha blood. Talk about trying to start a fight. They know damn well that's all that gets your attention this time of year, and the women who have appointments would kick their asses for even daring to draw your eye."

126

He sighed. It seemed every year more females showed up in town, hoping to hook up with him or his brothers. They tried to bypass the agreements his father made with other packs with the appointments. "Great."

"Yeah. I lied and said all you guys had paired up already. You want shocking?" She jerked her thumb toward a far corner. "See the two redheaded males over there? You'll never guess where they've come from."

"I'm not in the mood to play games."

"They have accents. They're Irish. They wanted to vacation over here to try out American wolf bitches. I don't know who to feel sorrier for since, they're kind of rough around the edges and our females tend to be a little too coddled. One of them hit on me." She grinned. "What do you think? Should I go for it?"

Anton grinned, glanced at the two burly men and studied them closely. "The one in the blue shirt would probably challenge you. He looks mean enough for you not to break him easily or scare him away."

"I was thinking about taking on both."

He chuckled. "Wolves aren't known to share well. They may fight over you."

"They're brothers. I figure they have to be used to sharing since they're from the same litter. They said they shared a woman's body once." She winked. "They can do it again."

"That's so wrong." He laughed though—couldn't help it. "Good luck. Don't do anything inside the bar. They look big enough to do a lot of property damage if you're wrong and they decide to challenge each other in an attempt to impress you."

"I haven't found any other prospects who appeal to me."

"What about Boris?" He remembered the Russian transplant she had spent the last few mating heats with.

"He had to go home. His father took sick." Depression settled on her features. "I'll miss him. I had a lot of fun with him and that wolf had serious sex skills."

"He didn't ask you to go with him?"

She waved it off. "He asked. He loves me but he wanted a mate. Can you see me being his alpha bitch?" She snorted. "I'd make all the pups in his pack wet their pants."

Sympathy welled inside Anton. "You'd make a good one."

"Been there and done that." She met his gaze. "Never again. Love sucks, and I'm just glad you took me in when I showed up here. This is where I belong."

He let it go. Glenda didn't talk about her past much but when she'd arrived in town, she'd been in bad shape. Someone had obviously abused her. She'd been half dead when she'd been found hiding inside a motel room, nearly unconscious. The Harris family had nursed her to health, accepted her into the pack, and Anton had personally trained her to fight. They'd been fast friends ever since, nearly family.

"How goes it with the she-cat? I think you've lost your mind, by the way."

"She's upset."

"I would be too, if I were a cat."

He shot her an annoyed expression. "She found out about how the packs send me women to test out."

"Oh. Yeah. If she's into you, that would definitely piss a woman off. Some don't like to share."

"I just want her." His voice dropped. "I feel things."

He wasn't able to block the surprise punch that slammed into his stomach.

He grunted and shot Glenda a glare while he rubbed the spot. "What the hell was that for?"

"Feel that? That's nothing compared to what your parents will do when they find out you're holed up with the enemy. Maybe I should deck you in the head to try to knock some sense into you. You're not thinking clearly."

"She's unlike anyone I've ever known."

"I bet. She's a *cat*."

"She's mostly human."

"That's two strikes against her then. Why don't you allow me to take her to a safe house? Two birds with one stone. She won't be upstairs under your dick and she'll be safe from the pups. I won't hurt her."

He knew Glenda would keep her word. It would be the perfect way to be rid of Shannon until he could track down the pups threatening her. He just didn't want to let her go yet. "No."

"Oh hell, Anton. Do you know what you're doing?"

"Not a clue." He sighed. "But wish me luck. I'm about to go upstairs and she's not going to be welcoming."

"Got her hackles up, huh?" She laughed. "A hissy fit? Maybe she's going to cough up a hairball and throw it at you?"

He playfully snapped his fangs at her, his eyes flashing. "Cute."

"I'm not the one infatuated by a forbidden pussy. I also think with the head on my shoulders."

Anton groaned and left the bar.

He had no idea how to handle Shannon's injured feelings, but he wanted to make it clear that he didn't plan on hurting her in any way.

Chapter Eight

Shannon paced. It left her unsettled to be alone inside Anton's home without him there after that werewolf woman had shown up. She'd studied the window and the area outside it but there wasn't a way to leave without dropping a good fifteen feet onto the pavement below. It would probably be painful when she landed if she tried to escape through that exit.

The door beeped and she spun in fear and frantically glanced around, searching for a weapon.

Anton stepped inside when the door swung open. He frowned at her, paused, and then quietly closed it firmly behind him.

"Did you find them? Is the problem handled? Can I go now?"

"No to all your questions." He watched her with those sexy eyes. "We should talk."

"I really don't see a reason for that. I should leave."

"That's not happening anytime soon. I have some of the pups looking for the ones who visited your apartment." He withdrew his cell phone from his back pocket to place it on top of the table inside the door. "They will call me when they've located them."

"Why are you being so stubborn?"

"I could lie but I don't want to. I'm not ready to let you go."

Shannon's heart started to pound. "Why not?"

"You know why." He reached for his waist, grabbed two handfuls of his shirt, and pulled it up to reveal his lean, fit, tan abdomen. "We're attracted to each other." He tore the material over his head, tossed it to the floor, and reached for his belt next.

"Speak for yourself," she lied. She couldn't help noticing his broad shoulders or those muscular arms. He had an incredible body. The best she'd ever seen. *Of course*, she remembered, *he's a werewolf who probably stays fit by running around in fur.* The thought threw cold water on her libido, a reminder of how different they were.

He bent, tore off his boots, and straightened, wearing just his jeans. "I thought we could talk and get to know each other better."

"I'm not having sex with you."

He stared at her. "Did I say you had to?"

"No but you're staring at me as though I'm a pork chop while you're removing your clothes. You look hungry."

A grin curved his lips and he licked them. "You *are* tasty." His focus lowered to her thighs. "But you're more like dessert to me than dinner. Sweet and sinfully tempting."

Her cheeks flamed. "You're being crude by reminding me of that. But I guess, as a player, you talk to women like that often."

All traces of humor disappeared from his features. "You really think I'm one?"

"Aren't you? Let's see. Your father sets up women to come fuck you every day. If the shoe fits, Anton…"

"Don't bait me, kitten."

"Don't call me that."

They watched each other until he sighed. "I don't want to fight with you."

"Good. Great. Let me walk out of here and we won't have to speak ever again."

"It's my duty as the future alpha to find a mate. The only way to do that is through spending time and having sex with females. I've been groomed my entire life to take this path. I have an older brother from a different mother but he's a half-breed. He refused to take the lead position when our father steps down. I never had the choice he did, with his human blood."

"Hear that?" She tilted her head. "Is that a violin playing?"

He growled. "That's heavy metal from the bar below us. I'm assuming you're being a smartass."

"I actually don't hear any music, and you bet I'm being flip. Am I supposed to feel sorry for you? You made your bed—and shared it a lot. If you want to get laid, find someone else. I'm not your type." She paused. "I'm not opening myself up to that kind of pain when I know tomorrow you'll just move on to the next person without even giving me a second thought."

"That won't happen."

"Right. I can't have sex with someone without feeling more than the sensation of their hands on me." She hesitated. "I'm being honest here, so listen closely. I was starting to feel things for you." She hated to tell him the truth but it would be worse if she didn't because he might keep trying to seduce her. "I really liked you."

"I knew that the second I smelled your pain. It wouldn't have hurt you otherwise, when you learned about the other women." He took a few steps closer. "Hurting you isn't something I want."

"Then put your shirt back on and stay away."

"I can't." His features softened. "I want you too much."

"You fuck women to see if you can mate with them. That would definitely leave me out of the running." She backed up until she found the corner of the room. "Stop it," she hissed when he stalked forward.

He paused. "I admit that it would be a shock if we turned out to be mates. My family would certainly never see that one coming. Hell, my parents would be horrified if they knew I wanted you, kitten. Your puma blood, even as faint as it is, would be a nightmare situation for them if something serious grew between us." He chuckled. "Yet, spending the rest of my life with you doesn't sound so bad."

"You don't even know me."

"It's emotions and chemistry combined. We've got that going."

Her heart raced and her breathing increased. Tears filled her eyes and she hated it. "Please don't do this."

All trace of amusement left him. "Don't do that. Don't cry."

"Don't hurt me then."

"You think I'm going to force you?"

"I…" She licked her lips. "I don't know, but when we touch, weird stuff happens to me. Just back off."

"What happens?" He watched her but didn't draw any closer.

"Just stuff." She refused to cry.

His features softened further, and so did the look in his eyes. "Kitten," he murmured.

"Stop that!"

He growled softly and suddenly dropped to his knees before her. Just feet separated them and he stared at her. "Come here. At least allow me to hold you. I'm groveling. I've never done that for a woman before. I can smell your pain again and I can't take it."

She pressed against the cool wall. "No. Keep your hands to yourself."

"Talk to me then. Am I threatening from here?" He sat back on his calves, spread his thighs, and planted his big hands on his knees. "What happens to you when we touch? We'll start there."

Shannon refused to tell him.

"I'll start then. At first I felt this huge wave of protectiveness when I held you. When I realized you were puma, I fought my wolf, who wanted to toss you away from me, but then it accepted you after a few deep breaths. I wanted you, and so did the wolf, Shannon. You make me ache with need. I want to breathe in your scent and touching you affects me so deeply it's a little frightening for me. I've never backed away from a willing woman before but I was afraid I'd hurt you. I'd do anything to avoid that. I'm even willing to protect you against *me*."

"Nothing has changed then." She glanced down at his lap and then back up. "You're still huge."

"I've had time to cool down and know what to expect this time. I'll be patient. I won't take you the way I would a bitch. You're *not* one. You're delicate and precious."

"Precious?" Her eyebrows shot up.

He actually blushed. "Yeah. I said it. I've never felt this way about a woman before. It's not bullshit or a line. I'm confused as hell but I'm here trying to figure this out. I don't run away when something scares me." He gave her a meaningful look.

"You think I'm cowering in a corner out of fear?"

He sighed. "The wall doesn't need to be held up."

"I'm confused but mostly I know I'm vulnerable. I gave up dating, Anton. It never worked out, no matter how hard I tried.

After a few failed relationships, I just stopped trying to have one. It wasn't worth the heartache."

"I don't plan to break your heart and I know the truth about you. I think you're beautiful, intelligent, funny, and I enjoy spending time with you. I find it sexy that you're part puma."

"That makes it worse," she admitted. "We haven't even gone on a date but we know there can't be a future for us. You're a werewolf and I'm part cat. The two don't mix."

"I would have to disagree with that statement. There's something strong between us, a pull we shouldn't deny. I am nearly obsessive about you and you're jealous over the idea of me with someone else. Admit *that* at least."

"It doesn't change anything."

"It changes everything," he rasped. "I have feelings and so do you. We haven't gone on a date yet, you're right about that, but we're ahead of all that already. You flee when you're scared and that's why you want to leave so bad. The idea of staying here with me and allowing me to touch you in any way frightens you. You're in denial if you believe there's only a physical attraction between us."

She hesitated, chewed on her lip, and a thought struck. "How much do you know about pumas?"

"Not that much."

"Maybe I'm ovulating." Hope soared. "That may explain how I react to you. Maybe that's it. I'm so human, my version of going into heat just makes me turned on faster and stronger than usual."

"Is that what I do to you when we touch? Do I make you ache?"

"Yes," she admitted. "It's stronger than anything I've ever experienced. Especially with the way you smell and when you nibble on me. Even those growls you make so often turn me on."

"How much more? Where do I rate on a scale of one to ten between the best human who has ever touched you and me?"

She hesitated. "He was maybe a four to your ten."

That drew a grin from him. "Are we talking about inches?" He looked down at his lap and then winked at her.

"Stop. I'm trying to be serious."

"I'm sorry. I thought you'd laugh. I'm glad you're not crying anymore. I really can't stand to see that. It tears me up inside to see your tears and I just want to hold you to make it better. I want to make love to you, Shannon."

"I don't want to be another notch on your bedpost and I really *will* get attached to you. I'm one of those dopey women who believe sex and love are one and the same. I don't really want to admit it because that probably sounds pathetic to you, but you can't have me without hurting me." She glanced at his lap again and then at his face. "And I'm not talking about just because you're thick and big down there. You asked me how long it's been since I had sex.

It's been years, Anton. Not since my last relationship ended. I'm not the casual type in any sense."

Surprise registered on his features at her confession, but just as swiftly anger simmered in his dark eyes. "Did he do something to you? Hurt you? It had to have been something horrible to make you swear off males for that long. Give me his name and I'll make him pay for whatever he did to you."

"It's not what you're thinking. No guy hit me or abused me. I'm different. I had to hide certain things from guys I dated. They sense it and I lived in fear that I'd accidentally reveal that I'm not quite normal. It took a toll eventually. It hurt me, watching them withdraw from me, but it always happened. They thought I either had affairs or I just didn't care enough about them. I just couldn't open up to them about what I am."

"What did you hide besides your ancestry?"

"My sex drive, for one." She blushed. "And don't look at me with that hungry look. I'm being honest because you asked. I usually had a higher one than the guy I dated and I had to refrain from scratching or biting. I'm afraid of spiders. Try to explain to a guy why and how you ended up on top of a wall unit because one scared you. I had to do that. I had to tell him I'd gotten up there to dust the top of it because that sounded better than saying my instincts drove me up there. He thought I was nuts but he'd heard me hiss and ran into the room before I could calm enough to climb down."

Anton chuckled. "Sorry."

"I've made weird noises in my sleep." She shrugged. "One boyfriend said I should see a shrink. He said dreaming I was a cat had to be a sign of mental issues."

"What made him believe you dreamed you were a cat?"

"I liked to grip and release my pillow the way cats dig their paws into things."

"You can bite and scratch me. If you knead things in your sleep, I won't ask you to see a shrink." He gave her a sincere look. "You don't have to hide anything from me. Isn't that worth taking a chance? I don't know what will happen between us but I'm here. I'm willing to see where this leads. Does that matter at all?"

"I really want to…but it's not worth the heartache I know I'll suffer just for a one-night stand."

The heartbroken look on Shannon's face twisted his gut. He made a decision instantly. "I'm offering you more than that. Stay here with me during the mating heat. That's a commitment I've never made to a woman before. Once it starts, I'll only want you. I'm even willing to mark you to ensure it."

"I don't know what that means."

Frustration welled. Her father should have found a way to ensure his daughter's survival better before he died. He should have found a pride who accepted mixed breeds to prevent her from being raised without any kind of support. The fact that she'd survived for so long before running into her enemy astounded him. She knew nothing about shifters or their ways.

"Marking you will mean I bite you and draw your blood. It's a way of staking my claim on you so my wolf knows, and so do others, that I'm serious about you. It's not a mating but you'll carry my scent and you'll be all my wolf craves."

"How do I know your wolf won't want to kill me?"

"Trust me on this. That's not what the other half of me wants. We're in total agreement about you. The only eating that will take place is the pleasurable kind."

He loved that she blushed. He'd never had someone so innocent, and while it terrified him a little, it excited him more. He made a mental note to try not to go too fast if he talked her into staying, not wanting to shock her by doing anything too over the top. *Treat her as though she's completely human,* he decided.

"I don't know what the future holds for us, Shannon. That's the same with any relationship but I've never hooked up with a woman for the entire time of mating heat. I've also never marked anyone before. That's a commitment I take very seriously. There's nothing casual about what I'm offering or how I feel about you."

He watched emotions play across her beautiful face. His heart pounded and his wolf pressed tightly against his skin. It wanted her so bad he had to fight it back. "I won't cheat on you. You'll be it for me during the heat. I'll need you like air and food. I'd go insane if you left me. *Crazy* insane. Shit, trust me on that. I've never wanted to make any form of commitment to a woman before. It's serious, Shannon." He decided not to tell her that, if she ran from him after he marked her, he'd go after her. He planned to make sure that didn't happen. "Please?"

Indecision and longing battled inside her. He offered her at least two weeks of total acceptance of what she was. No hiding anything. No having to hold back the way she'd always had to do with other men. Was it worth the risk of getting her heart broken at the end of whatever werewolf mating heat was? She needed to consider that.

A fierce werewolf sat before her, begging for her to stay with him. Anton wasn't the type to do something that drastic unless he really meant what he said. She had no doubt he'd never offered any kind of commitment to a woman before. That had to mean a lot. She desperately wanted to trust him.

She stared into his beautiful eyes and saw sincerity there. She nodded before she chickened out. "I'm afraid but you made some good points. I don't want to regret not giving us a shot."

He smiled and lifted to stand on his knees. His arms rose. "Come here."

She hesitated and glanced at the bed. "I can't sleep there with you. I don't want you to compare me to any of the other women you must have shared it with."

He softly cursed and rose to his feet. "That would never happen but I understand. I have a fold-out couch. It's new, never been used, and I have sheets that are brand new." He nearly ran to it, tossed off the cushions, and opened the queen-sized bed. He went to a closet, grabbed pillows and pale blue sheets, and made up the bed. He threw a denim comforter on top and faced her. "See? No one has ever slept here. It's just ours."

That was sweet. "Really?"

"Smell the things and you can tell they're new. I told you I just redid the apartment. New couch, new sheets, pillows, and even the comforter. My bed is a king-size. My stuff wouldn't fit on the smaller mattress."

She walked closer to him. "I'm nervous."

"Don't be. We'll take it slow." He reached for the front of his jeans and then stopped. "I'll leave them on for now. Yeah. That's a good idea."

"Condoms."

He nodded. "Right." He launched himself toward his dresser, moving fast, and tore the drawer open so quickly it came totally out of the compartment that held it. Boxes of condoms hit the floor. He softly cursed.

143

Shannon grinned. "I guess I'm not the only one nervous."

He peered over his shoulder and gave her a sheepish grin. "I want to do this properly. I don't want to scare you. I'm also concerned about marking you."

"Will it hurt?"

He hesitated. "Not if I do it correctly. Don't worry. I've heard advice about how to mark a woman." He put the drawer back into dresser, then bent over to grab a large box of condoms. He turned, holding them.

"That's an awfully big box."

"I *really* want you."

She had to look away from him while she bared her body. Her cheeks were warm, she knew she blushed, and she hoped he still found her attractive. When she stood totally naked, she found the courage to look at him.

Anton had sunk his teeth into his bottom lip and the box gripped in his fist had become a little crushed. Raw hunger radiated from his dark gaze, now locked on her breasts. A soft growl rumbled from him and then he lifted his gaze to hers.

"You're going to kill me."

"I am not."

"Trust me. This slow thing...I'm never going to survive. If you only knew what I wanted to do."

"What do you want to do to me?"

He took a deep breath. "Tackle you, lift your ass into the air to put you on your hands and knees in front of me, tear open my jeans and fuck you until I collapse." He shook his head. "But I won't. Lie down for me on your back, Shannon."

The sheets were cool to the touch when she climbed onto the mattress. She turned and stretched out. The smells coming from around her assured her he'd been honest. The sheets and pillowcases didn't smell of laundry soap but instead held that out-of-the-package-newness scent. It didn't surprise her that a guy wouldn't wash stuff before using them. She'd lived with men before. The humor actually made her smile.

He groaned, tore open the box, and she saw his hands tremble when he tore off a roll of condoms. He paused. "I should put one on now. No. I'll wait. If I take my jeans down, I don't think I could zip them back up."

She focused on the front of his jeans—the rigid, thick bulge pressing against the denim proof that he wanted her. Her focus returned to his face and the humor struck her. She laughed. "You look more anxious than I am."

He flashed a grin. "Probably. I'm your first shifter so the pressure is on for me to make this great for you, and this is my first time marking a woman."

"Take deep breaths." She held out her hand. "I'll hold the condoms."

145

He passed them over to her. "Here."

"You think we'll need all these?"

"Yes." He dropped the box on the floor next to the bed and put his knee on the edge of the mattress. "I'm gearing up for mating heat and my hormones are going a little crazy."

His warm hand brushed over her thigh. "Spread wide for me, kitten."

She hesitated and then did it. She knew her cheeks pinkened, since she'd exposed her pussy to him, but the low growl he made assured her he enjoyed the sight as his gaze fastened there. He licked his lips, his nose flared as he took in her scent, and he put his other knee on the bed and faced her. She watched as he slid down the bed to sprawl on his belly until his arms braced him in the cradle of her thighs. Their gazes met.

"You have no idea what you do to me. I could get addicted to you."

She shivered at the thickness of his voice, how it deepened into a harsh, rough sound. "Just hearing you talk to me in that tone makes me ache."

"Talk to me. Tell me if I move too fast, frighten you, or if you're uncomfortable."

"Okay. What about this marking thing?"

He hesitated. "I won't warn you but I'm hoping I time it perfectly so you'll barely notice. Trust me."

"I'm spread out naked on a bed with you. If that isn't trust, I don't know what is."

He chuckled. "Good. Relax for me, kitten. This will feel good."

He slid his hands under her ass, his shoulders lowering to press against her thighs, and focused on her spread sex, just under his mouth. Shannon closed her eyes and her fingers fisted. The crinkle of the condom wrappers reminded her that she held them so she placed them on the pillow next to her and then grabbed the edge of it as a hot, firm tongue slid across her clit.

Her breath caught in her throat and a snarl tore from Anton. She jolted from the vicious sound but then he sealed his lips around her sensitive flesh, suckling and licking at her furiously. Ecstasy arched her back and she would have bucked her hips if his hands weren't gripping her ass to keep her in place. He mercilessly dominated her clit. She moaned and purred, the sounds tearing from her throat, and she clawed at the pillow.

She knew she was going to come embarrassingly fast again, but Anton seemed to sense it, because he pulled his mouth away and lifted her ass a little. She gasped when his tongue penetrated her vagina. He surged forward, entered her, and snarled again, working his tongue deeper inside her body.

"Anton," she rasped.

He withdrew and pushed forward again, his tongue feeling long and thick as he explored her, fucking her slowly. His nose

147

rubbed her swollen, throbbing clit each time he drove into her, his face pressed tightly against her folds. She tensed, her eyes snapped open to stare at the ceiling, and she screamed his name when the climax gripped her.

A groan came from Anton as he kept moving his tongue inside her, seemed to coax her pleasure out longer, and then he withdrew. His cheek rubbed the inside of her thigh with a slight rasp. She felt his lips there when he turned his head, and then something sharp and wet dragged against the tender skin. He moved up a little, brushed light kisses over the curve of her lower belly, all the way to the top of her hip.

He struck fast, just as her body started to relax from the intense pleasure he'd given her, and his fangs sank into the fleshy part of her hip just under the bone.

She gasped, her hand released the pillow to grab his thick, silky hair, and she clutched his head. Pain and pleasure surged through her body at the sharp bite, confusing her senses. His tongue laved the area he'd bitten and another deep groan came from him but was muffled against her skin. His jaw worked gently to squeeze the skin he held between his teeth.

She focused on the ceiling. The pain faded but she knew his teeth remained. He'd bitten her. She knew he'd planned to mark her but she hadn't expected it just yet. He eased the hold of his mouth and licked her skin. He brushed a few kisses on the spot before lifting his head to check on her.

His eyes had shifted into that exotic look of part wolf, part man. They were beautiful and incredibly dark. Passion burned in his intense gaze and he licked his lips, drawing her attention lower. Blood—hers—covered his lips. Her hands released their hold on his hair.

He growled low at her, removed all traces of her blood with a few more swipes of his tongue, and then rose up to his knees.

"You're marked and mine for the next few weeks." His tone came out even harsher, gruffer, and less human. "Hand me a condom. I'm in control."

She turned her head and found where they'd ended up. Her fingers shook as she tore one from the roll and handed it to him.

He used his teeth to rip it open so he only had to use one hand. His free one tore at the snap of his jeans. He spit the piece of wrapper away and met her gaze again.

"Close your eyes. I don't want you afraid. Just feel."

She hesitated. "Do you want me to turn over?"

"No. I don't trust myself to take you that way yet. My wolf gets a little too excited in that position."

"What's not to trust? Will you be too rough?"

He met her worried gaze. "The condom will prevent me from mating you. If I were to come inside you and bite you at the same time, you'd end up with me forever."

Her jaw dropped.

He softly growled. "I won't bite while I fuck you, Shannon. But the condom would prevent me from accidentally mating you even if I *did* get you with my teeth. I'm just being careful. Your taste drives me a little insane."

"In a bad, want-to-maul-me way?"

He flashed a grin. "No. In an I-want-to-fuck-you-like-an-animal-and-mate-you way. I'm in control though. Close your eyes and trust me."

Shannon closed her eyes. She heard the denim whisper down his legs, the mattress moved as he kicked free of his jeans, and she thought she could even hear him roll on the condom. She wanted to peer down between their bodies to get a glimpse of his cock but then he lowered over her and the opportunity was gone once their bodies were pressed together.

"Look at me," he demanded.

His voice turned her on and the warm, hot flesh pressed against her did too. She inhaled his scent and her stomach clenched with need. She didn't hesitate to wrap her legs around his hips high enough to curve her legs over his ass. They stared at each other for long seconds.

"You're so beautiful," he rasped. "I want you to know that."

Her mouth parted to tell him how she thought he was the most handsome man she'd ever met, even with his exotic, wolfish eyes at the moment, but his mouth descended quickly to mute any words.

There was no gentle brush of lips. Anton's hungry mouth branded her, and not even the taste of her own blood could stop her from responding with her own frantic desire that built lightning fast.

His growl vibrated against her puckered nipples and his hips lifted enough to spread her thighs wider apart. She couldn't miss the hard, thick brush of his condom-covered cock as it nudged her soaked folds. He didn't use his hands, didn't need to in his deeply aroused condition, and then when he found the perfect spot, he pressed forward.

She gasped against his tongue when the thick crown of his cock slowly penetrated her pussy. He stopped kissing her but didn't move his mouth away. They both held their breaths a little before he groaned, pushing in deeper but going really slowly as he stretched her wider to accommodate him.

Shannon clutched his shoulders, her nails digging into his skin, but she forced her grip to ease. She had to remember not to claw during sex, a desire she always had if she experienced pleasure, and Anton gave her just that as her body parted for him, regardless of the snug fit. He pressed deeper and she moaned again.

When he started to withdraw, her legs instantly tightened to prevent him from leaving her body but then he pushed forward again, driving deeper, moving back and forth as he made her take more and more of him. Nothing had ever felt so pleasurable.

He backed up a little and she met his gaze. "Don't hold back. You can't hurt me. Just don't draw blood with your teeth. I'm not sure how pumas mate so we'd better not risk it."

She stopped trying to fight the urge to dig her nails into his skin. He gasped and then growled at her, his sexy eyes narrowing, and he gave her a pained smile. She froze.

"It feels good," he assured her. "You're so tight. Am I hurting you?"

"No."

"Hang on to me. My control is starting to slip. I've been a saint so far."

She wasn't sure what that meant until he buried his face against her throat and started to move again. His hips pressed against her inner thighs when he drove forward, giving her all of himself, and she gasped at the sensation. The overpowering jolt of desire made her want to bite him but she turned her head away instead, clenched her teeth, and then he started to pound against her fast and hard.

The hammering speed of his cock against her highly sensitized nerve endings inside her pussy nearly hurt, but it was too good to be pain. She panted, purred, and then screamed when she came apart under him. Explosions of ecstasy cascaded from her center straight into her brain and Anton snarled a word she didn't catch, threw his head back, and roared out in a half howl, half cry. Inside her, he seemed to swell and pulse within her twitching vaginal muscles.

Their heavy breathing drew Shannon back from the happy place the big male on top of her had sent her to. She turned her head, realized he'd mostly collapsed on top of her but his braced arms allowed her to breathe and sweat slicked their bodies. Anton lifted his head from the pillow next to hers and met her gaze. The exotic wolf look of his eyes had gone, replaced by the fully human Anton.

He smiled at her, showed her his perfectly straight, human, white teeth. "I didn't hurt you, did I?"

"No."

"Good. I'll give you about two minutes and then we're going again. I'll allow you to pick the position. Got any favorites?"

She stared at him in shock. "Seriously?"

"I'm not human. Neither are you, totally. Tell me you don't want me again and I'll stop." He suddenly lowered his face, brushed his nose against her shoulder, and growled deep in his throat.

Desire shot through her at the slight touch and the sound he made.

He chuckled. "That's what I thought."

Chapter Nine

Shannon laughed and threw the wash cloth at Anton as she tried to duck under his arm. He grabbed her around her waist, hauled her off her feet, and pressed her back against the cold tile on the wall of the shower. He looked highly amused when he pinned her there, his hips snuggled between her slippery thighs, and on instinct she wrapped her legs around his hips. He shelved her ass on his forearm to hold her in place so she didn't slide down his soapy body.

"Wash your own butt."

He chuckled. "You're supposed to worship me."

"I am, huh? Is that some funky shifter rule?"

"Nope but you have to admit, after the night we spent together and all the pleasure we shared, you think I'm a god."

"Really? Why would you say that? Someone has gotten a little egotistical."

"It may have been all those times you called out 'oh god'." He brushed a kiss on her chin, lifting her higher. "Weren't you telling me something?"

Shannon laughed. She couldn't help it. The night she'd spent with Anton had been the best one of her life. It had been more than just sex. He'd made love to her. Every touch, every kiss, every caress they'd shared had bonded them in ways she'd never experienced before. Her smile faded a little at that realization.

"What's wrong?" He pulled back.

"Nothing."

A soft warning snarl tore from him. "Don't lie to me."

She stared into his eyes. "I'm not."

"You are. Do you think I can't feel it? I'm very attuned to you. I could feel you emotionally pulling away from me as if you'd done it physically."

That stunned her. "Seriously?"

He answered by watching her silently.

"Okay. I was just..." Her gaze lowered to the top of his shoulder where she gripped him and noticed the faint but healing claw marks where her nails had marred his skin.

"Just what?"

"It's stupid."

"I doubt I'd agree. Why are you withdrawing from me? Did I say something wrong? I'm kidding about the god thing. You don't have to wash my ass and I don't expect you to worship me."

She lifted her gaze to meet his. "I know you were teasing. I just think that last night might have been too intense."

"You're sore. I'm sorry." He eased her down onto her feet. "I forget how human you are."

"I'm fine. My muscles ache a little but that's not it." She ran her hands over his chest, using the water falling over his shoulder to wipe away soap. "I meant emotionally. You touch me in ways that only guys I've been seriously involved with do. I don't know how else to say it."

"We're involved."

Frustration rose as she glanced at him. "I meant it must be a shifter thing but the way you touch me confuses me."

The blank expression on his handsome face assured her she'd lost him.

"Damn," she muttered, staring at his chest again. "You touch me like a guy who isn't a one-night stand."

"You're more to me than that." He suddenly gripped her chin and forced her to meet his gaze. "You're mine."

For a few weeks, her mind whispered. "You marked me. I'm still not sure what that means."

"It tells other males you are mine and I'll do anything to protect you. You'll carry my scent. It also makes my wolf know we're together, that the connection is solid."

"I carry your scent?"

"Saliva from my fangs entered your bloodstream when I bit you."

"How long does that last?"

"A few weeks." He drew back but kept hold of her chin. "Does that bother you?"

"No." She hadn't realized how tense he'd become until he relaxed.

"You're cranky in the morning before breakfast, aren't you?" He released her to turn away into the full spray of the shower to rinse off. "I'll order food to be brought up while you finish showering. Hurry up. It won't take long. I'm starving and I bet you are too."

Her stomach rumbled as if on cue. Anton chuckled, ducked his head under the water to rinse away the conditioner, and then shook his head. Water sprayed her. He opened the shower door and stepped out before she could wipe the water off her face to retaliate. She could see the silhouette of him as he used a towel next to the frosted glass door to dry off. She hesitated and then reached for his shampoo.

Emotions confused her. She had a really bad feeling that if the next few weeks were anything compared to the last twelve hours, she'd be walking away from Anton without her heart intact. He was easy to love, and the sex... Instant desire stirred her body at just the memory. Her nipples hardened despite the warm water cascading over them and she knew she'd never be able to get enough of him.

I have to be in cat heat or something. It would explain a lot. First, how she'd jumped into a sexual relationship with a werewolf so

157

quickly, and how her body ached just thinking about him touching her again.

She had to leave the bathroom wearing just a towel five minutes later. Anton sat at the bar, wearing a pair of black sweatpants, his long hair still damp, and he turned to stare at her when she stepped closer to him.

"Mind if I borrow some clothes?"

"I do because I like you naked, but I don't want whoever brings breakfast up to see you in so little." His head jerked to the dresser. "Help yourself."

"Thanks."

She avoided the condom drawer he'd managed to put back into place and he had cleaned up all the spilled boxes from the floor. She chose a pair of drawstring shorts and a big black metal-band T-shirt from his clothes. She knew he watched her when she dropped the towel to dress but refused to meet his gaze until she had something on.

"I have to go to a pack meeting in half an hour." He glanced at the wall clock inside the kitchen area. "I won't be gone long. After I eat, I need to—"

Someone kicked the door. Anton got to his feet and walked toward it. "Breakfast."

Shannon backed up. The last time someone had come through that door it had been that werewolf woman. She hoped another one

158

hadn't shown up to make threats. The door opened and the blond guy stepped inside holding a tray. He nodded at Anton and then turned his gaze on Shannon to run it slowly down her body.

A vicious snarl made the guy yank his attention from Shannon.

"Don't look at her, Yon," Anton threatened.

Yon paled. "Shit."

"Give me the tray and leave."

"Why are you acting so nuts? I'm not hitting on her."

Anton grabbed the tray. "Leave." The order came out harsh and scary sounding.

The muscular blond stumbled back, hit the corner of the doorframe, and softly swore. "You marked her, didn't you? You're acting nuts. You didn't mind me being near her yesterday."

"Keep your mouth muzzled and I only want you to deliver food to her. My business is no one else's. Are we clear?"

"Perfectly." Yon fled.

Shannon's eyebrows arched at the strange interaction. Anton kicked the door closed, turned with tray in hand, and scowled at her. "What?"

"Nothing."

"I'm sorry. Now I'm the grouchy one. I didn't like him looking at you."

"Was I in danger?"

159

"No." He strode to the counter. "I feel very possessive of you. It's got to be the marking thing." He slammed the tray down. "I guess it makes me a little crazy. I just wanted to punch him for even daring to glance your way."

"Wow."

"What?"

"Your fangs are showing."

"Sorry. Damn." A hand lifted to feel his sharp points and then it dropped to his side. "Marking is scary stuff. I heard it was bad but I really wanted to knock him down the stairs. He thinks you're attractive."

"He didn't say anything."

"He didn't have to. His nose flared and his eyes darkened. Trust me. He thinks you're sexy and would love to touch you." He paused. "And I didn't like it one bit."

"I'm not interested in him. Does that help? Blonds aren't my type."

"Are werewolves?"

"Well, no. At least not until you."

"Good." His fangs receded and he seemed to calm. "Let's eat. I'm sorry I have to leave you alone. Once the heat starts we take a break from most things and I'll have some time off. Not much work gets done this time of year."

160

She took a seat next to him at the counter. "Shifter holiday, huh?"

A chuckle escaped him. "At least for werewolves."

"So the bar downstairs will be closed?"

"It will be this year. Last year my brother kept it open and lost a lot of money due to repairs."

Shannon gave him a curious look.

"We get pretty aggressive when we're horny. Not a good mix when you've got a bunch of single werewolf males, with fewer females to try to impress enough to allow the males to fuck them. We also get a lot of out-of-town visitors from smaller places who are looking to find women to hook up with during the heat. There were a lot of fights. I'm running things now and have decided to close the bar once the mating heat starts. They can battle it out in the woods instead of inside."

"Don't the humans around here notice anything weird or suspect what you are?"

"It's an annual thing that's gone on forever. They just assume it's a busy tourist season. They sure don't mind the money it brings in. We eat a hell of a lot and fill up the motel down the street."

"A rowdy tourist season."

"Yeah." He grinned. "But we keep away from the humans for the most part. I'll have to work a few nights during the heat but I won't be gone long."

"You have another job besides running the bar?"

"I'm a Harris, and this is our pack. We patrol at night to make sure no visiting weres go after any local human women. It's been known to happen despite it being against our laws. We're never to do anything to risk humans discovering what we are. My brothers and I have split shifts with some of the pack enforcers. Of course, we own a lot of land that's private property for the runnings, to make sure humans don't accidentally stumble into that."

"What are those?"

He hesitated. "I don't think you want to know and I'm not going to be a part of it, so it's nothing for you to be concerned about."

"Now I'm *really* curious."

He picked up his fork, his attention on his food, and took a bite. Shannon waited for a response, not eating. She watched his throat work as he swallowed.

"That bad, huh?"

He finally looked at her. "It's for single weres. At night they go into our woods and run."

"That's not so bad."

"To fuck."

"Oh." Her cheeks warmed. "Got it. Kind of like chasing a female."

"Kind of. Yeah. Chasing goes on. Fights."

162

"And? I suspect it's more than that."

"It's a free-for-all, okay?" He finally met her gaze. "Think werewolf orgy."

To avoid his gaze, she focused on her food as she picked up her fork. "Do you ever attend them?"

The silence stretched. "I went to a few before I was expected to find a mate and that shit with my father started, when he began making the schedule for me to meet women from other packs."

"I see." She really didn't. The idea of him going to a running made her a little sick at heart. It sounded a little disgusting to her way of thinking.

"It's a good way for males and females to hook up, test each other out to see if they're possible mates. Humans have spring break. Tell me a lot of sex isn't going on then."

"True."

"Ever go to spring break?"

"No."

They ate in silence until Anton stood. "I have to go to that pack meeting and then I have some errands to run. Yon will bring you lunch in a few hours if I'm not back yet. Don't talk to him."

She gaped at him.

"I didn't mean that the way it sounded. He's starting to feel the mating heat. He's not hooked up with anyone either. He knows I marked you but hormones make any male stupid. I just don't want

163

you to be polite to him and have him believe you would welcome any advances. We're not human. Remember that."

"I promise to glare at him." She smiled. "How is that?"

Anton surprised her by leaning over to brush a feathery kiss on her forehead. "Perfect. You're safe here. Make yourself at home. I have cable and every channel. Just don't leave."

"I won't."

He backed up, studied her closely, and then seemed assured she meant it. He spun away and walked to the dresser. She watched him pull on a tank top and socks. He sat on the edge of his bed to shove his feet inside boots then gave her a grin before he strode out the door.

Shannon's shoulders slumped after he left. She closed her eyes, trying to determine if she felt any different since she'd been marked. It obviously affected Anton but she didn't sense any changes in herself.

* * * * *

Anton snarled at Carl, holding the pup above the floor, and everyone inside the room watched him in stunned silence. "I told you to leave her alone."

The pup paled. "She's just—"

"Under my protection." He snarled, shook the pup, and slammed him against the wall. "I see your friends aren't here. Were they too frightened to face me?"

The pup frantically nodded, his eyes wide with terror.

"They should be. I want you, them, and the rogues you took to her place at the pack meeting tree in an hour. If you make me hunt you down, I'm *really* going to be angry. You don't want that. I'm just going to yell, issue orders, and make threats. Make me track you down and there will be blood. Am I clear?"

"Yes," the pup whined.

Anton dropped him. "Run. Find them and be there."

Elroy Harris prowled closer to his son, a look of danger glinted from his dark gaze when Anton faced him, but curiosity showed as well.

"What was that about, son?"

"Could we talk alone?"

Elroy frowned. "No. You just threatened to bloody a pup in a roomful of pack. If he's done something that drastic, we all need to hear about it."

"Fuck," Anton hissed. "This is a private matter."

"Not anymore. You made it public by grabbing him here."

"Fine. The pups kidnapped a woman and took her into the woods to hunt her." He crossed his arms over his chest and shot a glare around the room. "I came across them after they'd treed her."

165

Gasps sounded and shock reflected on a lot of faces. Elroy cursed. "Is she well?"

"She's fine. She's a good climber and I got there in time. I warned them to stay away from her. Then I discovered Carl and a few of the pups disobeyed me by entering her home with a few rogues. They totally destroyed her apartment."

"Apartment? They aren't private or secluded from humans. Why would a female be living in one? Does her pack own it? I'm going to need to contact her alpha to make peace. When did this happen? Why didn't you tell me?" Anger made Elroy growl the words.

Anton hesitated, hating to admit this to his father, unsure of how he'd react. "She isn't a werewolf." He hoped that would be enough but doubted it. His father was thorough about learning every detail when an incident took place with a pack member. "There's no alpha to calm."

"Shit!" Elroy spun to glare around the room. "We have pups going after humans? Who hasn't taught their young not to do this?" He shot a particularly cold look toward Carl's uncle. "Do I need to take this up with your brother, Ed?"

The guy paled. "We taught our young to follow the rules. I don't know why Carl did it but it won't happen again." The guy bolted from his chair. "I'll see he's at the meeting tree myself."

Elroy spun. "Is the human well? How much did she understand? What did she see? Is she going to contact the police or did you have to kill her to assure our safety?"

Shit! Anton took a deep breath. "She's human but not totally."

"What does that mean? She's a partial were? Where's her family?"

"Her father was half human and half shifter. He died when she was a small child and she's been raised by her totally human mother. She can't shift. She just faintly carries the shifter scent. It's why the pups attacked her and kidnapped her to hunt."

"I am going to kick their asses! We don't force females to have sex even during mating heat. That's pack law."

Anton knew he couldn't avoid it any longer. He was surprised his father hadn't already heard the complaint from the Mortell alpha after he'd spurned his daughter's advances in favor of Shannon. "They didn't want to fuck her. They wanted to kill her." The shocked look on his father's features assured him he needed to keep going. "She's part puma...and under my protection," he added quickly.

There. I said it. He waited for the explosion from his father.

It only took a few seconds for Elroy to recover from the shock. "What?" he yelled.

"She's mostly human, Dad. Helpless. She can't shift. She's without anyone to protect her. It seems cats kill half-breeds so her

167

father had to flee from his pride. She didn't ask for this trouble. Our pups accosted her in the parking lot of a grocery store outside of our territory, kidnapped her, and wanted to kill her. She's this tiny thing, sweet as hell, and didn't ever do anything to deserve that shit."

Elroy paced, rage gripping his features, and claws shot from his fingertips. He halted finally and gave Anton a grim nod. "I understand. So the pups went against your order to leave her alone? Did they harm her when they showed up at her apartment?"

"She's fine. She wasn't home when they tried to find her."

"You said rogues?"

"Two of them were inside her apartment with our pups. It seems they're hanging with a few of them."

"Unacceptable!" Elroy shot another glare at the pack members assembled inside his living room. "Rogues are lawless. What are pups doing hanging out with them? See the trouble this causes? They defied a direct order from their future alpha." He glanced back at Anton. "Give me her address and I'll post one of the elder mated wolves at her place until we deal with this situation, to make sure it doesn't happen again. We also need to determine if she's at risk from these rogues. They may have told others. I'll assume she's hiding in the outskirts of our territory, since I'd know of her presence otherwise."

"It's been taken care of," Anton hedged. "She's safe."

"Who did you assign? He'll need to be old enough not to be affected by mating heat."

Damn. Anton groaned silently. "I didn't. She's staying with me."

Dark brown eyes widened and Elroy's lips parted. "What?"

Anton squared his shoulders. "You heard me. She's staying with me. She's under my protection, inside my home." While he was admitting things that would send his father into a rage, he may as well confess the rest. "I marked her. She'll be staying with me through mating heat."

Elroy lunged.

Anton tensed but his father didn't attack. Instead, he grabbed his son and shoved his nose against his throat, inhaled deeply, and then snarled as he leapt back, releasing him. Pure rage transformed his father's features as his shifter genes slid into place. Fangs elongated and the shape of his eyes narrowed enough to show his wolf. The brown of his irises turned completely black.

"I smell her on you. Even that damn cologne can't camouflage it. You really marked a *puma*? What the hell is wrong with you? That's just..." He obviously grappled for words.

"Sick," a pack member hissed.

"Demented," another added.

"She must be a hot piece of pussy," someone snorted.

A few laughs sounded. Elroy snarled and shot a warning glower around the room before he glared at Anton.

"Why would you do that? Explain to me how you could do such a thing?"

But anger boiled inside Anton and he took a threatening step toward the male who'd insulted Shannon with the pussy remark. He flashed sharp fangs at the man and allowed his claws to slide out. He knew his face changed, since fear etched on the other man's features.

"Anton!" Elroy snarled.

It halted him from going after the male, and he softly growled at his father. "You don't have to like it or agree with it. I don't need your permission to find a female to spend my mating heat with. Rave has agreed to take over the schedule you set in place with the females from other packs. If anyone goes after Shannon, threatens her, or insults her in front of me again," he shot the offender another murderous look, "there will be hell to pay. She is under my protection and I'll kill anyone who poses a danger to her." He met his father's stunned gaze. *"Anyone."*

Elroy tensed. "I'm your alpha and your father. Are you threatening me?"

"She's under my protection." Anton didn't bother to try to mute the anger in his tone. "She's *mine*. That's all I'm saying.

Anyone who attempts to harm her will deal with me." He took the time to meet every gaze in the room. "I'll kill for her."

"It looks like you were remiss in teaching your sons not to fuck the enemy," one of the pack members muttered.

Elroy moved before anyone could react. He took the male who'd spoken down to the floor, tore into his arms with his claws, and the man howled in pain.

Elroy snarled, inches from his terrified face. "What did you say?"

"Nothing," the bleeding male whined. "I'm sorry, Alpha Elroy. It was just the shock." The male twisted his head to reveal his throat, the only sign of submission he could offer while pinned flat on his back. "My humble apologies."

Elroy released him and stood, wiping the blood from his claws on his jeans. He kept away from Anton. "Go. We'll discuss this later. I'm sure your mother will have some things to say as well."

Anton flinched. His mother made his father seem like a lovable little puppy. He fled the house he'd been raised in to go meet the pups at the woods. If they didn't show, he'd tear them up. The urge to harm something hummed through his veins. Mating heat was growing strong inside him, turning him more aggressive, and he'd even threatened his father. They both realized it.

An image of Shannon flashed through his mind as he started his motorcycle. She'd gotten under his skin, into his blood, and had

171

become an obsession. He wasn't sure it was just because he'd marked her. There was just something about her that called to every part of him.

Would I really kill someone I love if it came down to protecting her? The question formed in his thoughts—and so did the answer. *In a heartbeat.*

He groaned, pulling away from the curb. *I think I'm falling in love, damn it.*

Chapter Ten

The blond werewolf, Yon, avoided her gaze when he walked into Anton's home with a tray of food for lunch. "Where do you want it?"

Shannon walked closer to him. "I'll take it."

He nearly stumbled backward to avoid her. "No! Stay back."

She froze and then retreated. "Are you okay?"

"I won't be if my scent gets on you." He glanced at her then. "Anton threatened to skin me alive if I got close to you, and he meant it. I've never seen him so nuts about a woman. But then, I can't remember him ever marking one before, either. Just tell me where you want this and I'm out of here."

She pointed to the bar that divided the living room from the kitchen. He moved quickly, put it down, and fled. The door slammed behind him.

Her eyebrows lifted. At least she didn't feel afraid. That had to be an improvement, since she'd been a little worried about being alone with the guy.

The smell of food drew her closer. The bar downstairs had an excellent cook. She sat and started to eat the burger and fries they'd sent her. She sniffed at the dark drink, recognized raspberry-flavored iced tea, and took a sip.

173

She'd nearly finished all of her meal when something bumped against the door. Her spine stiffened, her attention fixed on it, and her heart started to race.

It suddenly opened, flung wide, and Anton stumbled inside. Seeing his torn shirt, blood on his cheek, and more smeared on his arms, alarmed her. She shot to her feet so fast the stool crashed to the floor. She noticed more blood as her stunned gaze traveled down his body.

Dark red stains smeared his jeans on the legs, thighs, and one ankle. His hair was a mess. He met her gaze with wolf-shaped eyes. "It's fine. Don't be worried. I need to shower."

"What happened?"

"I met two of the rogues who broke into your apartment." Broad shoulders shrugged. "They didn't want to listen to me. They aren't a threat anymore."

Shannon gaped at Anton, and the blood staining him. "You…" She couldn't say the words.

"Fought to the death? Yes," he answered softly. "I told you I'd kill to protect you. I'll be back." He limped toward the bathroom.

"You're hurt."

"I'll be fine. I heal fast."

He didn't spare her another look but instead entered the other room, closed the door firmly behind him, and in less than a minute the shower came on.

The food inside her stomach churned. Anton had killed someone for her. The fact that he'd said rogues—plural—made her feel even sicker. He might have had to kill more than one werewolf. She yearned to go after him to make sure he wasn't really hurt but the closed bathroom door assured her she wouldn't be welcome. Indecision left her standing there with a feeling of helplessness.

The front door suddenly flew open again, but this time it was a woman who stormed inside. She drew to a jerking halt when she spotted Shannon. They stared at each other. The woman appeared to be in her late thirties, had long dark hair to her waist and brown eyes. Her lips parted, fangs flashed, and a snarl came from her mouth.

"You!"

Fear gripped Shannon. "Who are you?"

"I'm Eve." The woman's face started to transform enough for there to be no doubt of her werewolf heritage. "I'm going to kill you!"

The woman lunged.

Instinct took over and panic struck Shannon. She bolted for safety—that being Anton. She hit the bathroom door with enough force to break the flimsy handle securing it to the doorjamb, grabbed the shower door without thought, flung it open, and jumped.

175

Anton twisted his body her way and barely caught her, his shock apparent. The vicious growl from Eve made him spin again to trap Shannon's body against the wall and one of his hands automatically shot out to strike the advancing woman in the chest. He shoved her and sent her flying out the bathroom doorway.

Shannon wrapped tighter around Anton, her body soaked from the water pouring down on them as well as from his slick, wet body. She buried her nose against his throat and shook from terror. She couldn't think beyond her need to cling to him, her instincts overriding rational thought. One of his strong arms wrapped tighter around her waist.

"What the hell is going on?" Anton yelled. "Shit! I just knocked my mother on her ass." He awkwardly bent, turned off the water, and stepped over the rim of the shower to glare down at the woman sprawled on the floor. "Mom? What are you doing here?"

Shannon turned her face just enough to watch the tall woman ungraciously get up from the floor. She staggered when she stood and then slowly turned to glare at her son.

"I came to kill *that*!"

Anton reacted instantly. He snarled, his fangs growing, and sharp points slid against Shannon's side where he gripped her. She looked down at the claws on his hands. He tried to gently pry Shannon off him but she wrapped around him more securely.

"Shit. You've terrified her." The anger in his tone made him growl the words. "You have no authority to come into my home after someone under my protection!" His other hand lifted and he rubbed his palm down Shannon's back in an attempt to soothe her fear. "I don't care if you're my mother."

His mother wanted her dead. Shannon digested that, her mind starting to work beyond the panic. Her heart rate slowed and she eased her hold on him but her body wasn't willing to release him entirely yet. She was starting to hate the way she lost control around werewolves. It was embarrassing. She clung to a naked guy in front of his mother as if she were a terrified child and Anton was a big teddy bear. *A sexy, wet one. But I bet I look pathetic.*

"That's what you've chosen to share your heat with?" Eve curled her lip in disgust. "Look how weak she is!"

"Actually, she's pretty strong. Her thighs aren't clamped around your waist, so take my word for it." His anger eased. "She's mostly human but when she's threatened or scared, her puma instincts hit. You obviously terrified her. Not cool, Mom."

"You humiliated me in front of our entire pack and you're chastising *me*?" Eve's eyes darkened to black. "They're all talking about my son and his cat."

Anton turned, grabbed a towel, and then sighed. "It's okay, kitten. Want to let me go? Stand behind me but I feel weird talking to my mom naked for this long. It's one thing to remove my clothes

177

to shift but we don't just hang out talking to each other while naked."

Shannon nodded and took a deep breath. She forced her body to listen when she demanded her hold on him ease. She slid on his slippery body to her feet but instantly took his suggestion. She moved behind him while he wrapped the towel around his waist. She pressed against his back as soon as he had it secured snug around his hips and peered around him at the tall werewolf female.

Eve growled low at her. Anton growled back louder. "Enough, Mom. I just got her down. Look at me."

Eve jerked her glare away from Shannon to give him the full measure of her anger. "I won't have it. You get rid of her."

"You don't give me orders in my own home."

"I'm the alpha bitch and your mother!"

"I respect you for both — but I go with her if you want her gone from the territory."

"Unacceptable! You're my son. I raised you better." Eve moved closer. "Either you will kill her or *I* will. That will end the rumors immediately. We'll say you were just using her to get information about those nasty rodent chasers. I can still spin this nightmare to save face."

Anton crossed his arms over his chest, watching his mother with narrowed eyes. "Not happening. No one is going to hurt Shannon, and I don't give a damn what the pack thinks. I understand you're unhappy but that's not my problem. You can leave now."

Eve paled. "I'm giving you an order! Kill the cat or I'll do it!"

"No." His arms dropped and he reached back to nudge Shannon a little farther behind him. "Don't make me pick you up and carry you out, Mom. How would *that* look to the pack? You aren't welcome here while Shannon is with me. If you ever threaten her again, you won't enjoy the reaction you get."

"Anton," the woman snarled, "I won't permit this embarrassment to continue. You will not do this to me!"

"I'm not doing *anything* to you." He stepped closer, his body tense, and his voice deepened. "You're the one who invaded my home to threaten the woman I marked."

Dark eyes widened with horror and Eve stumbled back. "What?"

"Marked. Made mine." He advanced another step. "As in I sank my teeth into her, shared my scent, my bed, my home. I couldn't care less if your bitch friends snicker over it. I don't give a fuck if the males make jokes." He kept advancing, forcing his mother to retreat into the living room. "Shannon means more to me than that. Now leave!" He yelled the last words.

Eve fled but not before she shot a lethal glare toward Shannon where she stood at the bathroom door, watching the scene unfold. Anton's mother slammed his door when she stormed out. He stared

179

at it until Shannon walked up behind him to place a trembling hand on the middle of his back.

"I'm so sorry."

He twisted to stare down at her. "For what?"

"You just argued with your mother over me."

He took a deep breath, his temper cooling. "She came here to start trouble. It's what she does best. You're not to blame."

"I'm still sorry."

His voice softened. "Don't be. I'm not. It's about time I stood up to her."

"What can I do?"

A black eyebrow arched. "Get naked? That would improve my mood."

"You're hurt." She'd seen the marks on his chest, one on his back, and on the side of his thigh when he'd stood naked in front of her. "You're still limping. Do you have a first-aid kit?"

"Strip for me. That will make everything better."

"But—"

"It's starting." He growled the words, then his tone softened. "Between the stresses I've been under, the fighting, and now my mother pissing me off, it's sped up the process. The mating heat is affecting me. I need you, Shannon."

She noticed that his towel had tented. She gazed at the rigid length of his cock pressed against the wet, thick material. "Oh."

"It's going to get bad." A hand lifted to his hair, shook some of the wet strands, and he bit his lower lip. "I'm almost afraid I'm going to hurt you. I don't want that." Frustration crossed his handsome features.

Shannon reached for her shirt. "You won't."

"Do you understand how much I'm going to need you? I've always been with other werewolves during this time, who are affected by it too. I don't want to frighten you but sex is all I'm going to think about and want when it's gripping me."

She tore the shirt over her head. "Okay."

His gaze lowered to her bared chest and he tore at his towel. "We have to use condoms."

"I know. You explained. Get them." She started to remove the rest of her clothes.

He nearly lunged for the drawer of the dresser. Her breath caught when he grabbed two boxes. She didn't say anything, instead headed for the pullout bed, which was still out, and climbed onto the middle of the mattress to stretch on her back.

The hunger on Anton's face turned her on while he admired every inch of her body. His cock swelled to an impressive size. She lifted her hand, crooked a finger at him and smiled while she bent her legs up. She spread them wide apart.

That was all it took. Anton threw the boxes on the bed next to where she waited and came after her. He didn't climb over her but instead stretched out on his belly between her spread legs and just buried his face there. The shock of his mouth on her pussy only lasted a second. He frantically nuzzled her, his tongue seeking and finding her clit, while his hands pushed her thighs wider to make room for him.

Shannon threw her head back in pleasure from the strong, quick flicks of his tongue lashing her sensitive bud. He growled. The sound made her hotter and she knew she wouldn't last long. Her belly quivered, her nipples puckered, and Anton grew bolder by pressing his mouth firmer against her folds. His soft growls turned into snarls, as if he were losing control. She understood since her own need skyrocketed. She blindly grabbed for the condoms, tore at the box, and used her teeth to rip open one of the foil packets.

He jerked his mouth away. "I need you." He didn't sound human anymore.

One look at his face should have terrified her. Anton's fangs had slid out and his eyes had darkened. She shoved the condom at him. He lifted his hands, showed his fingernails had grown into sharp claws, and she sat up. She had never put a condom on a man before. How hard could it be?

She gripped him with one hand at the base of his shaft, tried to steady the center of the condom over the thick crown, and started to

182

roll it down. Anton growled at her. She hoped that didn't mean she had done it wrong. She released him, threw her body back and reached for him.

"I'm ready." She knew she was soaked with need. She could feel the dampness against her thighs. She ached to come.

Anton dropped over her, careful not to rake her with his nails, and his cock bumped against her ass. She wrapped her legs around the back of his thighs, adjusted her hips, and he pressed against her pussy. He slid along the seam of her sex and frustration twisted his features. She reached between them when he lifted up a little, guiding him to the entrance of her pussy, and he pushed inside.

She cried out and grabbed his hips. She marveled at the wondrous sensation as he stretched her with his rigid length, filled her, and met her need. "Yes."

He braced above her with his arms to keep his chest from crushing hers and then started to move in deep, strong thrusts. Shannon cried out his name over and over, her hips matching his frantic ones, and used her hold on him to meet his pace. Sweat beaded their bodies, helped them move together, their skin rubbing, sliding where it touched. The ecstasy built inside Shannon, her vaginal walls clamping around him, and she screamed his name when pure ecstasy shot through her.

Anton threw his head back and moaned loudly as he started to come. She could feel his cock throb inside her body as his hips slowed and he pressed deeply into her. He shook from the intensity

183

of his release. When the strongest spasms started to ease, he collapsed on top of her. Both of them panted.

He was heavy but she had no urge to complain. Shannon grinned. Sex with Anton just seemed to get better and better. She didn't protest until she needed more air. She released his hips to push on his chest. He lifted up just a little.

"Did I hurt you?"

"No." Shannon met his worried gaze, still smiling. "That was amazing."

The worry faded from his eyes. "Good, because this is just the beginning." He wiggled his hips and withdrew from her body to toss the spent condom away.

She hated when they separated. She'd felt connected to him, as if they'd been one.

"Hand me another condom and roll over."

"Again? Now?" She didn't hide her astonishment as she handed him the condom.

He rose to his knees between her parted thighs, tore open the condom with his now normal hands, and looked down toward his waist. Her gaze followed where he stared. His cock hadn't softened.

"Mating heat. Get used to this sight because this is how I'm going to be for the duration." He met her gaze. "I have about a minute recovery time."

"Okay. I hope I can walk when this is over."

He chuckled. "I'm strong enough to carry you around if you can't."

She laughed, pushed up with her arms, and backed up on the bed as he rolled on the condom. She rolled over, going to her hands and knees, and spread her thighs. She looked over her shoulder to back up until her ass flashed in front of him and her legs brushed the outside of his.

"Is this how you want me?"

"Yes."

She winked at him. "So what are you waiting for? Need an invitation?"

His hand curved around her hip, slid over her belly, and his fingers found her clit to tease. "Are you sure you aren't sore? I was rough."

"No. I want you, Anton. I've never wanted anyone more. You don't need to worry about me, okay? When you touch me, do that growl thing. You have no idea what it does to me."

He gripped his cock, inched forward to nudge her pussy, and slowly entered her a few inches but then stopped. Shannon bit back a moan and resisted closing her eyes to just enjoy the sensation of him inside her again. She didn't want to look away from him.

"What does it do?"

185

"Makes me ache. My nipples tighten so much it hurts. My stomach does funny things and I feel hot all over. It's almost as if you set me on fire."

His free hand caressed the curve of her ass. "Are you sure you're not going into your own heat?"

She contemplated that. "I don't know."

He continued to play with her clit and gently rocked his hips to enter her a little deeper and then withdrew. Shannon closed her eyes, clawed the covers, and let her head drop lower. Her elbows bent to brace against the bed and she just let the sensations overtake her. She started to make a sound that should have startled her but what Anton did felt too good for her to care or want to contemplate it.

He started to move faster, his hips slapping against her ass, and made his own soft, animalistic sounds that turned her on more.

Passion gripped Anton so fiercely, it hurt. His cock and balls had never been so tight or needy. Shannon was vibrating around his cock, her scent of arousal stronger than anything he'd ever experienced with any woman, and the smell drove him crazy. He wanted to fuck her until he couldn't move.

"You're purring for me, kitten," he rasped. "That's such a turn-on. Don't stop."

Her pussy seemed to squeeze him, or maybe he'd never had that much blood rush into his dick before. Either way, her sleek heat tightened around him until he had to fight to move inside her and not come at the same time. His finger pressed tighter against her clit, strummed it frantically, knowing he couldn't last much longer.

She screamed out his name and her muscles gripped him so tightly, he came. Pleasure nearly tore him apart from his balls out as he filled the condom with his release. He bent over her, his fangs tingled, and he focused on a spot on the curve of her shoulder. He salivated, his wolf howling from within, and before he knew it, her blood coated his tongue when he bit into her.

Shannon's body jerked under his, her vaginal walls quaked, and the haze of rapture flooded him. He came more, his hips jerking violently, and he couldn't stop for anything as he kept fucking her, still coming, and his teeth sank in deeper to assure his wolf she wouldn't leave him.

A muffled sob finally penetrated his mind and horror struck him at what he'd done.

He forced his jaws apart, released her shoulder, and threw himself back to separate their bodies. He nearly fell off the end of the bed in his haste to put distance between them. The wound he'd inflicted showed his teeth marks, welling with bright red blood. Shannon's small body shook but she didn't move otherwise.

"Shannon," he rasped, her blood on his lips, all he could still taste as he reached out to her. The second his hand brushed her back she collapsed to her side, panting. He froze. "I'm sorry. I didn't mean to bite you."

She didn't respond. Her hair hid her face from him but she remained curled on her side, blood smeared on his bed from her shoulder, and he didn't know what to do. It shocked him that sex had turned into violence. He touched her again but she didn't react. He saw her chest rise and fall but the sounds had stopped coming from her. He crawled toward her to brush her hair back from her face to see that her eyes were closed.

"Shannon?"

She didn't respond. Panic gripped him. Had he hurt her that bad?

"Shannon!" He yelled her name.

She jerked, her eyes opened, and she did the last thing he expected.

She smiled at him.

"Wow. That's the first time someone has made me pass out."

He gaped at her until he could form words. "You were crying."

She stretched her legs a little and reached for him as she rolled to her back. Her fingers brushed his cheek. "No. I don't know *what* sound that was but it sure wasn't pain. Can we do that again?"

"No. I bit you."

She used her other hand to reach up, touched the spot, and then winced. "Ouch." She glanced at her hand, saw the blood and paled.

"I just thought you nipped me. I didn't know you drew blood. Is it bad?"

"I don't know. Don't move."

He jumped from the bed to rush inside the bathroom and grab a wet washcloth. He rushed back into the bedroom to find her seated on the middle of the bed with a curious expression. It stunned him that she wasn't afraid of him after his attack.

"It only hurts when I touch it. And it feels warm. Don't look so upset. I'm fine."

She tried to comfort him and it made him feel worse as he circled the bed and sat down behind her. Her red hair had touched the blood sliding down her back from the bite. He'd really tagged her good. He gently lifted her hair out of the way to press the cloth against her delicate skin. She winced and he felt worse.

"I'm so sorry," he rasped.

"It's okay."

"No. It's not. I really got you good."

"Why did you do it?" She peered at him with pure innocence.

Anton had to clear his throat. "I lost control." He couldn't meet her gaze anymore so he tended to her bite.

"Do you need a muzzle from now on when we have sex?"

He jerked his gaze up, astonished when she grinned at him, making a joke. He wasn't in the mood to laugh. "No. I tried to *mate* you, kitten. My wolf tried to, anyway, and I didn't stop him." He looked down at his lap, examined the condom, and blew out a breath. "It didn't break. We're okay."

"Oh." Her gaze skittered away to stare at something to the left of him. She looked back. "What do you mean, your wolf wanted to mate me?"

"My wolf wanted to keep you for good. I'm so sorry. I wasn't thinking."

"It's okay. I just thought you were marking me again."

"I did."

He tried to mask his emotions. He'd definitely made sure she'd carry his scent, and he'd tied her to him even stronger. No way would his wolf settle for any other female during the mating heat. If she left him, his wolf would go insane, track her down, and could hurt her. He didn't want to share those facts, afraid he'd scare her, and now he really needed her to want to stay. Worse, that mark would last longer than mating heat. He could feel her blood changing him already, forming a deeper bond—and he could sense his inner beast's contentment with that.

"No harm done." She gave him a brave smile. "I'm fine."

"I'm sorry."

"It's really doesn't hurt," she assured him.

He lifted the damp cloth and hid a wince. It wasn't some love bite just to mark her. No, he'd scarred her so she'd always carry his teeth impressions on her pale skin. He may as well have just

190

become engaged to Shannon. Bites that deep implied a pending mating. It was a sure sign of commitment when a male scarred a female with his bite.

Calm down, he ordered his wolf when it pressed against his skin, wanting Shannon again. He got the bleeding to stop and bit his tongue enough to draw blood. He hovered over her and licked her wound. She startled a little but then relaxed.

"It will help it heal faster," he murmured between licks.

"It's turning me on," she whispered. "I don't know how you do this to me but I want you again. I almost hurt from the need..."

He muffled a groan. It seemed his sexy little kitten was going into heat with him. How he'd make it through mating heat without forever binding them seemed a daunting task at best. He just needed to keep control.

Yeah, good luck with that. His dick stiffened painfully.

He removed the used condom and reached for another.

Chapter Eleven

I really purr, Shannon thought, digesting that concept as her throat hummed, her chest vibrated, and Anton continued to stroke her back. She'd woken up sprawled on top of his large body and to the strange noise she hadn't identified until her foggy brain cleared.

"I love that sound and your reaction to me touching you."

She lifted her head and the noise stopped. Anton smiled at her. She couldn't help but return it.

"Morning."

"Sore?"

She assessed her body. "No. I'm…" Heat warmed her cheeks. "I'm turned on again."

"You're definitely in heat too."

"I don't understand this. I've never gone into it before."

Anton continued to rub her back, brushing his fingers and palms over the curve of her ass and then up her spine. "I've been thinking about that. I believe I know why."

"Good. Clue me in because it's freaking me out a little." She didn't want to lie to him and she really wanted an explanation. "I'm a little frightened too. It's as though I don't know my own body anymore."

"You've lived around humans entirely since your father died. After you met me, your puma instincts have reacted more than they probably ever needed to before."

"Yeah. It's humiliating."

That drew a frown from him and his hand paused. "Why?"

"I always thought I was pretty tough. Now I leap on you or climb trees whenever I get really scared. Think about it. Your mother, as an example, probably thinks I'm pathetic. A werewolf would have growled at her or something. Not me. I ran to you and practically knocked you down in the shower."

His body bounced her as he chuckled. "I think it's adorable."

"You're not the one always trembling and so scared you can't think. It's like a switch gets hit, my brain shuts down, and next thing I know I'm off the ground clutching you or on top of something. I tell myself to stop it, to get down and be brave, but my body doesn't listen."

"You're part puma and I'm a werewolf. My kind usually kills yours. It's natural for you to flee and seek higher ground. It's a strong instinct, ingrained in your genes." His hand rubbed her back again. "Hell, sometimes I see rabbits and take a few steps before I'm able to stop myself. I want to chase the things down and eat them. I've been dealing with what I am all my life and still fight those impulses."

"Really?"

"Yeah. I could share all kinds of embarrassing things I've done while I adjusted to being a werewolf."

"Like what?"

"In high school, I decided to date this cute human. I liked her and she was hot. I was fifteen and hormonal. I asked her out, bought flowers, and was really nervous because I wasn't sure how humans interacted on dates. She answered the door holding her pet cat. That thing went insane, hissed at me, panicked, and it bolted out the door. I was after it faster than you can imagine. It ran up a tree and there I stood under it, trying to think of a way to get it, when Sally rushed out to see what was going on. I had to hide my face. I'd started to change. I couldn't talk because our voices deepen. She thought I was a freak and mean for scaring her cat somehow. I just walked away, so add rude on top of all that. She avoided me and glared daggers at me every time we crossed paths in the hallways until she moved away two years later."

Shannon smiled. "Sorry."

"Then there was the first pack run I attended after I started to become a man—as in noticed women and knew what a sex drive was." He paused. "You probably don't want to hear this one."

"Go ahead."

He actually blushed. "Imagine a hormonal teen on his first run with the pack. We strip down by the meeting tree to shift and there were all these naked women. I got a boner from hell and realized

194

everyone would notice. I couldn't take off my pants. It's considered rude to react that way unless it's mating heat. This was just a pack run, which we do monthly to celebrate the full moon. It's kind of our version of a holiday and a way for the pack to do something together. My father knew why I stood there, not stripping down, and ordered me to go home. As I was walking away, my father yelled out for me to jack off before I came to the next one. I wanted to die on the spot."

Shannon's mouth dropped open. "He didn't!"

"He totally did. I will never forget the laughter and how I ran all the way home. I didn't speak to him for two days. It embarrassed me enough that I never wanted to go to another one."

"Your dad sounds like an ass."

"He believes it's toughening us up to do shit like that." He sighed. "There's no shame in your fear of werewolves, Shannon. On the food chain, we're something to be afraid of." He suddenly grinned. "I bet you've never had a mouse problem."

"No." She suddenly laughed. "I never thought about it, but in my first apartment, all the neighbors complained about field mice during the summer but I never had any inside my place."

Anton grinned. "You scent faintly of puma. Those mice would have avoided you at all costs."

"So you think being around you is helping my shifter blood kind of come forth?"

"Yes."

She closed her eyes and tried to imagine a large cat. She pictured claws and a tail.

"What are you doing?"

She sighed and opened her eyes. "I can't shift. I just tried."

"Do you know how?"

"My mom asked my dad how *he* did it. She told me to imagine changing, to picture a large cat, and it would happen the way it did for him. It never worked though."

"Honey, if you could shift, you would have when you were terrified. Just because you're displaying some traits doesn't mean you can transform. The fact that you're only a quarter shifter pretty much guarantees you won't be able to."

"Oh." She wasn't sure if she should feel disappointed or not.

"It doesn't matter, and hell, I'm kind of happy you can't. If you had claws and shifted into a cat when you jumped on me the way you do..." He chuckled. "You'd probably tear me up every time a werewolf gets close enough to trigger your fear."

"I'm not afraid of *you*."

He suddenly rolled them over to pin her under him. "Your scent is driving me crazy." He scooted down a little and dipped his head to open his mouth over her breast.

Shannon arched her back to lift the tip more firmly against his face. When he started to suckle, she moaned. Her stomach fluttered

196

and she knew moisture instantly dampened her thighs, which she tried to spread apart to make room for his hips.

"Please don't tease. I ache."

He released her nipple with a drag of his teeth. "You're so responsive."

"I'm dying for you."

He threw a hand toward the edge of the bed and searched for one of the condoms that had been dumped there during the night, but he cursed instead and looked away from her. "Where are the rubbers?"

"I think we knocked them off the bed before we passed out after that last round."

He moved off her and peered over the edge of the sofa bed. "Found them!"

"Hurry up." Shannon rolled over and got on her hands and knees. "Take me this way. You have no idea how good it feels when you take me from behind."

"I know." His voice deepened as he retrieved a few packets and turned to face her. A snarl tore from his mouth at seeing her waiting for him. "I—"

Someone pounded on the door. "Anton! Come quick! Your father has been hurt!"

Anton dropped the condoms and leapt from the bed to rush for the door. Shannon grabbed at the tangled covers and had barely wrapped them around her when he threw the door open to reveal a tall man she'd never seen before. The stranger panted, out of breath, and looked as though he'd run some distance.

"What happened?"

"I don't know." The guy leaned against the doorframe heavily. "Your mother called, said you weren't answering your phone, and said you were needed. Your father has been seriously injured. They're at their house."

Anton spun around, fear etched on his face, and looked at Shannon. "I have to go. I'll be back."

"Of course." She nodded. "Go."

He just threw on clothes, didn't even bother to put on shoes, and ran out the door with the other man. It slammed behind him but she heard it beep, assuring her he'd at least remembered to lock it.

Her body ached for him, burned, and guilt ate at her for it. His father had been hurt and she still wanted to have sex with Anton.

She took a few deep breaths and then decided a cold shower would help. Worry followed her into the bathroom. She prayed his father wouldn't die or that Anton wasn't in some kind of danger. Something or someone had severely hurt his father. She didn't know much about werewolves or what threatened them. Whatever happened, whatever the outcome, she knew she'd be there for him when he returned.

* * * * *

Anton shifted in the parking lot with Paul. They both ran toward the woods half a block down the road to reach his parents' house faster. He wasn't in any condition to drive. Worry and fear drove him to push past his usual endurance. He ran for miles and finally spotted the house. The door stood wide open and he just rushed inside.

"He's downstairs," his mother yelled from the back of the house. "Something attacked him. Hurry up! I think he's dying."

His wolf howled out in rage. Whoever had hurt his father would die. He nearly knocked his mother over when he raced through the hallway and skidded down the stairs. The smell of his father's blood filled his nose, leading him through the basement apartment to one of the holding cells they kept there. He saw a bloodied, partially covered figure curled into a ball on one of the cots. He wasn't thinking, just reacted, and rushed inside.

He shifted fast, panting, and reached for his father, but the second his hand touched the blanket, other scents filled his head.

Human and death.

He tore the covering off to stare in shock at an elderly human. The guy's throat had been torn open and unseeing green eyes stared at the wall.

The metal cell door slammed closed behind him and Anton turned.

199

His mother glared at him from the other side of the bars, backing up to remain out of his reach.

"You really thought I'd allow this to happen? That I'd let you to do this to me?" She bared her teeth at him. "You brought our *enemy* into our territory."

Understanding dawned. "Let me out of here." He grabbed the cell door and shook it. Metal rattled but the lock held. They'd been reinforced to contain werewolves who needed to be caged. "What have you done to Dad?"

"You mean the blood?" She gave him a cold smile. "I tore up his back during sex and rolled him to let his blood seep into the blanket while I kept him occupied. I knew the scent of it would make you rush into the cell. You males are so stupid, single-minded, always think with your noses or dicks."

"You killed this human? Why?"

"I needed a body." She shrugged. "It's just some homeless guy. No one will miss him."

Anton gaped at her. "It's against our laws."

"So is fucking the enemy!" she yelled, rage distorting her features. "So is humiliating your parents and your entire pack! I raised you to be a leader. Instead you betray me—and for what? A little cat whore?"

"She's under my protection. If you harm Shannon, I'll kill you."

Eve paled. "I'm your mother. Don't you *ever* threaten me again."

"She's mine."

"She's the enemy!"

"Not to me." He rattled the door. "Let me out of here. Where is Dad?"

She waved her hand. "He's in the woods, waiting for me. He has no clue. Sometimes a mate has to do tough things for her pack."

"If you harm Shannon," he snarled, "I *will* kill you. You'll stop being my mother and *you'll* become my enemy."

"She's no longer your concern."

"I've marked her." His mind started to work around his fear for Shannon's safety and his rage at being tricked by his mother. "I'll go insane without her. You'll have to kill me. Are you willing to go that far? Your mate and other children will never forgive you."

"I've thought of that. You haven't hit full heat yet. I'm going to have you drugged." She shot a distasteful glance at the dead body dumped on the cot. "I plan to shoot you with sedatives and once you're unconscious, I'll return to take it away. I've hired an outside doctor from another pack to come in. We'll keep you in a coma until the heat passes and he'll hook up a feeding tube and fluids. I told him you marked a bitch who died—which is partially true. She won't be alive much longer. By the time you wake up, she'll be out of your system."

"I swear to you, if you harm Shannon, I'll kill you!"

"I'm not going to lay a claw or fang on her." She chuckled. "I realized when your father said you'd threatened him that you'd feel obligated to kill whoever snuffed out that little rodent eater. "I'm just having her removed from our territory. No werewolf will harm your precious pussycat."

Anton tried to break the lock on the door again, his muscles straining. "If anything happens to her, I'll hold you accountable, you vicious bitch!"

"That hurts." She pouted. "Sometimes, as a mother, it's my job to do what's best for my children. I won't allow you to screw up your life or your position as future alpha of this pack. I've waited a long time to see my son take his rightful place and I've suffered a loveless mating that will end soon—when your father has an *accident*."

Horror jolted Anton. "What?"

"I only mated Elroy to be the mother of a future alpha. He never loved me, and he's so stupid he doesn't even realize how much I've grown to hate him over the years. He's too soft. He allowed that half-breed bastard of his into our territory when he should have killed Grady the second his pathetic human mother dumped him on us! Even *she* knew trash should be thrown away. Then Elroy allowed that bastard to mate a human! It's not right, and my mate doesn't bother to consider what I want or how it made me feel to know he would never kill that bastard to make me happy!"

202

"Grady is my brother." Anton started to pant, fighting the urge to transform. His wolf wanted to tear his mother apart. It didn't understand the bars would contain it but he did. "And my father...you're planning to *kill* him too?"

"Both of them are useless to me." She shrugged. "They are *weak*. You'll be a better alpha for the lessons I'm about to teach you. Never show your enemy mercy. It's kill or be killed. We're werewolves, not puppies."

"You're sick and demented."

She shrugged. "But I'm cunning. You're locked up, your father is out in the woods waiting to fuck me, and at this moment, that pest *you* fucked is about to be removed from our territory."

Anton's gut twisted. "What have you done? Who's going after Shannon?"

"I called the local pride leader. He was very interested to learn about her." Eve smiled coldly. "It seems they had no idea of her existence. He was more than happy to come tag and bag your pet."

"*No!*"

"Yes." She backed up into another cell, bent, and withdrew a weapon from underneath a pillow on the cot. "I'd love to stick around to watch you suffer a little longer after what you've put me through recently, but your stupid father will get impatient if I don't show up soon. He's always demanding sex." She lifted the tranquilizer gun to point at Anton's chest. "The doctor will arrive

203

tonight before this wears off. I'll have cleaned up your cage by then and your father believes I want a romantic vacation at our cabin by the lake. He won't find you. I'll keep him there." She winked. "'Night, sweetheart."

Anton leapt away from the bars but he had nowhere to hide. Pain stabbed his shoulder. He grabbed the dart and jerked it out. Dizziness struck him, despite how quickly he'd removed it, and his knees collapsed under him. He crashed painfully to the concrete floor, his mother's laugher filling his ears.

Shannon would be helpless, unprotected, and in danger. He fought the drugs but everything turned black.

* * * * *

Shannon had just taken a soda from the fridge when a knock sounded on the door. She started a little and stared but didn't go near it. Anton would just walk in. Yon also could enter the apartment. Whoever stood on the other side of the door could be dangerous.

It could be another woman sniffing after Anton, she thought. She remained still, held her breath, and hoped they'd just go away.

They knocked again.

She didn't move until something hit the door. She saw the frame shake. Another loud blow made wood snap as the door buckled. Terror gripped her and she dropped the soda, her gaze darting around the room, searching for a weapon or a way to escape.

The door gave completely under the third assault. Two large men entered, both of them just over six feet tall, blonds, with tanned skin. Their matching green eyes and features assured her they had to be brothers or closely related. Both men examined her while her heart hammered. Fear kept her immobile.

The one on the right sniffed and smiled. "Hello, little red. Don't bolt on us. We're not werewolves. Smell."

She just stared at them, terrified. They obviously believed she could tell what they were if she sniffed the air. Her mouth opened but nothing came out.

The one on the left frowned. "I don't think she can. Smell the humanness of her?"

"I mostly can't get over the stink of dog, Mark."

The other one snorted. "Damn. They *do* reek."

Mark cocked his head, other holding very still while he regarded Shannon. "I'm Mark and this is my brother Adam. We're puma shifters, and we've come to save you from the mangy mutt holding you hostage."

"Please leave," she managed to get out. "I don't need to be saved."

Adam made a face. "Brainwashed maybe?"

"Or stupid. Maybe she's so human she's useless to us."

"No. Try to get past the reek of dog. Smell that? She's in heat. She's coming with us if she's blooded enough to have that trait."

The other brother laughed. "And cute."

"She *is* good-looking. That's a plus." Adam took a cautious step forward. "We're not going to hurt you. We're taking you home with us."

Shannon backed up, trapped inside the kitchen, and shook her head frantically. "No. Leave me alone."

Her instincts were failing her. The urge to climb didn't hit her and when she tried to rush at the counter to get over it, speed didn't kick in, the way it usually did. One of them grabbed her as she struggled to scramble over the top. His hold around her waist hurt when he shook her and hissed.

"Don't fight me."

"Let me go!" She kicked at his legs and clawed at the skin of the arm securing her.

He turned with her suspended in his arms. "She's going to fight. Do it."

Mark moved in front of her and she watched in horror as he drew back his fist. She tried to twist in Adam's arms to avoid the blow but pain exploded into the side of her head. She didn't even get the chance to scream.

Chapter Twelve

"Anton? Wake up, damn it!"

The familiar voice had him struggling to fight off the groggy haze that engulfed him. A hand slapped his cheek and his eyes opened. He stared into his cousin's face, inches above his own.

Brand frowned. "What happened? Why did you kill a human?"

Anton tried to think around the fog inside his head. *A dead human? What the hell?*

He realized he lay sprawled naked on a cold, firm surface, and when he turned his head a little, he recognized one of the holding cells in his father's basement.

"I...what happened?"

"Fuck if I know." Brand gripped his arm and shoulder, forcing him to sit up. "I came here to talk to Uncle Elroy, found the front door locked, which was weird since it's always open, and tried the basement door to make sure everything was cool. Instead I only smelled blood and death when I came inside. I found you passed out cold, locked in this cell. Did you go nuts? There's a dead human two feet from us. Did you two fight?"

A face surfaced in his memory. A woman, a pretty one, with long, curly red hair and bright blue eyes...

His heart raced and he suddenly remembered everything as it clicked into place.

"Help me up."

"I'm trying. I'm not sure if I should have unlocked the door or not. Are you nuts? Did you have some kind of breakdown?"

"My mother is going to kill my father and Grady. She's gone after my woman, too."

"Shit!" Brand gasped, struggling to help Anton up. "So you killed the human trapped in here with you?"

"My mother did it. She used the blood scent to lure me inside the cell." He got to his unsteady feet, swayed, and knew he'd have fallen on his ass if his cousin's arms weren't supporting him. "She drugged me."

"I can tell." Brand had to half drag him outside the cell. "What do I do?" He helped Anton into the apartment area of the basement.

"There are drugs stored inside the cabinet by the cells. Find a green shot, not a red one. Give it to me."

Brand dumped him on the couch and darted back toward the cells. Anton gripped his head, the room spun a little, and he fought to remain conscious. It seemed to take an eternity before Brand crouched before him, holding up a green syringe.

"This one? What the hell is it?"

"Naloxone. We keep it and narcotic sedatives here. Shoot me directly in the vein. It will counteract the other."

"Sounds dangerous. Let me call for help."

"No time. It works lightning fast." Anton tried to reach for the syringe but his hand missed by inches, his equilibrium off. "Fuck. Just stick me."

"Fine." Brand used his teeth to tear off the plastic tip from the needle and stuck it in the big vein at the bend of Anton's elbow.

Within a minute his sluggish body responded. The drowsiness vanished. He took some deep breaths and focused on the task at hand.

"What do you want me to do?"

"Get me a phone."

Brand withdrew a cell phone from his back pocket and held it out. Anton grabbed it, careful not to crush the thing in his hand since anger was pumping him up, and dialed Rave's number. He got the machine.

"Pick up, Rave. It's an emergency. Stop fucking and grab the phone."

Seconds later an out-of-breath Rave answered. "This better be super important."

"Mom is going to kill Dad and Grady," he spoke quickly. "And she's sent someone after Shannon. Maybe more than one. They're going to be pride. Get to my apartment and protect my woman right now! Mother drugged me and locked me up. Brand is with me. I'll call everyone else. Get to Shannon *now*!"

209

"Is this a joke?"

"*No!*"

"Fuck!" Rave snarled.

"Go to her, damn it. She's alone."

"I'm going." Rave hung up.

Brand straightened, rushed to the closet that contained an assortment of clothes and pulled some out while Anton dialed Grady's number. Mika, his mate, answered on the second ring. "Hello?"

"Put Grady on the phone."

"He's in the shower. Which one of you is this? I can't tell you brothers apart on the phone." She laughed.

"This is Anton. Mom is planning to kill Dad and Grady. Just tell him to watch his back and protect you. This isn't a joke. Stay there or go somewhere safe but don't trust that bitch." He hung up before she could respond.

He dialed Von and Braden but neither of them answered their cell phones. He left them curt, detailed messages, telling them what their mother had set into motion, and asked them to go to his place to protect Shannon. He barely remembered to warn them that she had puma blood so they didn't freak out when they smelled her shifter genes, if they had missed hearing the rumors.

He hung up and realized Brand gawked at him.

"Don't," he threatened. "Yes, she's mine."

210

"I heard you'd hooked up with a woman but nobody said she was a cat shifter."

"Part." Anton managed to stand now, his legs steady under him, and jerked the clothes out of his cousin's hands. "She's mostly human and it doesn't matter to me if you approve or not."

"I didn't say anything negative." Brand seemed to recover from his stunned state. "I can't believe this is happening. I know your mom is mean and she's done some crappy shit over the years, but Uncle Elroy is her mate."

"It seems she hates him."

"Can't you call your place and warn Shannon?"

"I turned the phones off." He snarled, jerking sweatpants up his legs. "We were starting mating heat and I didn't want to be interrupted. Mom sent a runner to escort me here, otherwise I'd still be at home. She said Dad had been severely injured. Didn't you smell his blood inside the cell too?"

"I just assumed you'd fought with your father when he put you there. Hell of a time for Aunt Eve to pull this shit. It's near genius. Everyone already hooked up for the heat is nailing each other, and the rest of the pack is either hunting for someone to hook up with or running in the woods for the free-for-all. It's going to be tough to track down anyone to find help. You said she sent pride after your Shannon? She had to have invited them into our territory and assured them it would be safe. Otherwise there's no way they'd dare come here."

"Yeah. I have no idea how many of them to expect, either. My brothers have to get their messages. They'll come. We all have to take turns patrolling. That means we check them often." He headed out the door with Brand right behind him. "I need your help. I can't shift yet and I need a ride home. I also need you to help me protect Shannon. We may be in for a hell of a fight."

"You know I'd do anything for you, and I never want to miss a good fight."

Brand jumped into the driver's side of his truck and started the engine while Anton took the passenger seat.

"Are you going to have a problem helping me protect a part-puma shifter?"

Brand threw the truck into drive. "In college, I fell in love with a human and spotted leopard half-breed." He cleared his throat. "I never told anyone that before. She just up and left me one day."

Anton's eyebrows shot up. "Seriously?"

"Yeah. I didn't give a second thought to us supposedly being enemies. I just loved her, man. God, it tore my heart out when I realized she'd run out on me. I wanted to mate her but I guess she didn't want to stand up to her family or our pack. I'll help you protect your puma."

"Thanks."

212

Anton closed his eyes, his body finally leveling off from the drugs in his system, never happier for his ability to heal quickly. The horror of the situation hit. His mother had always been cold, remote, and not the best influence, but mates didn't kill each other. He'd thought his father put up with too much from the woman—it had always been a bone of contention between them after her poor treatment of his older half-brother Grady—but she actually planned to kill two people he loved.

Three. She was going after Shannon as well.

His cousin drove down the street, breaking every speed law their city had. Anton gripped the door as the truck took a turn too fast.

He loved Shannon. No doubt about it. Somehow it had finally happened, after all the years he'd tried to find a woman to mate. He'd enjoyed sex with other women but none of them had made him *feel*. He'd suspected he loved Shannon, had started to adjust to the idea, but now that she faced danger, he knew how deeply that love ran. He'd go insane if something were to happen to his sexy little kitten.

The bar came into sight and he spotted Rave's motorcycle parked in front of the building. Some of the tension eased. Shannon wasn't alone anymore. Brand locked up the brakes behind the bike and Anton jumped out before the engine died. The front door to the bar had been kicked in but he didn't give a damn how Rave had

213

gained entry to reach Shannon and protect her. He could replace a door, but never her.

Brand was right behind him when he pounded up the stairs to spot another door Rave had kicked in. He nearly slammed into the back of his shirtless, shoeless brother, standing just inside his apartment, only wearing jeans. Rave spun to face him, snarled, and his claws shot out until he saw who was behind him. He barely missed nailing Anton in the face, his claws missing his throat by mere inches.

"I was too late," Rave's grim voice informed him. "The doors were kicked in. I found blood on the bed, hers by the scent, but it's not fresh." He paused. "She's gone, Anton. They took her. I smell two pride males."

Anton threw back his head and howled his rage. A hand gripped his shoulder from behind. He turned his head but it wasn't Brand. His youngest brother, Braden, stood behind him. Von had arrived as well. All three males had matching furious expressions.

"They took her." Anton snarled the words. "They kidnapped my Shannon."

"We'll get her back," Rave swore softly. "There's only one pride close to us. I've scoped their territory in the past. I sometimes have to hang out at a biker bar that borders their lands. There's a lot of rogue activity there and I keep an eye on it for the pack to make sure they don't cause us problems."

214

Braden hesitated. "Are you sure they kidnapped her? Maybe she returned home with them willingly. What the hell were you doing with one of them?"

Von growled low. "Be quiet, Braden. I heard Rave say he found her blood on the bed…?"

"That's my fault," Anton admitted. "She's mine. I marked her. She wouldn't leave with them if given a choice. She's terrified of them."

"They aren't her pride?" Von calmly met his gaze.

"She's alone. She's mostly human, had been warned they'd kill her on sight for being as human as she is, and I'm the only shifter she's ever spent time with." Anton turned to study the apartment. He didn't see any signs of a struggle or damage except the broken door. He sniffed, the scent of two pride males, something he memorized, and rage gripped him again. "I'm going to tear them apart if they've killed her."

"Easy." Rave spoke softly. "She's pretty. They aren't going to kill her."

Brand shouldered a few of his cousins aside and sniffed near the bed. He softly cursed. "She's in heat. I'd know that scent anywhere."

"Oh fuck," Rave groaned. "That's worse. We have to find her fast."

Anton closed the distance between them. "They have some policy about killing the weak. Shannon said her father fled his pride because of his half-human blood. They wanted to kill him for it."

Rave took a deep breath and met Anton's gaze. "I know a lot about the cat shifters. The good news is, they won't kill her—at least not on purpose. The bad news is, they only kill weak males. The females?" He paused. "I don't want to tell you the rumors I've heard about that subject. You'll go nuts."

Anton crowded him, enraged, and demanded, "Tell me what you think they'll do to her. Don't make me ask again."

* * * * *

Shannon really wished she had remained unconscious as she assessed the dire situation she'd woken to. Seven male pride members stood around her in the woods. All of them were grim, scary guys ranging from their early twenties to early thirties. The two brothers who'd kidnapped her were among them.

Mark appeared slightly older than his brother Adam. He spoke as though he were the one in charge as he argued with another male. "She's too human for anyone to want to mate with."

"I'd take her," a blond twenty-something male offered. "Our women are scarce."

"They won't be if we were able to breed a lot more of our kind." Mark shot a glare at Shannon where she'd been dumped on

216

her ass in the grass with her hands secured behind her back. "She's a rare find."

"Her scent trace isn't known. Her blood parent wasn't from our pride." Adam moved next to his brother. "I'm with Mark on this. No mating this one. We know what needs to be done."

"I agree," a tall brunette sighed. "Besides, no male could harm his mate the way she'll suffer. She has no family in our pride to protest her treatment. She is a rare find that we must use to full advantage."

Shannon cleared her throat. "I'm no threat to you. Please just let me go. You'll never see me again. I can promise you that. I've never told anyone what I am. You don't have to kill me."

They ignored her. "I can't get past the stink of her though," one of the males whined, his voice grating. "She reeks of wolf."

"Hold your breath then." Mark shot him glare. "I've decided."

The blond who'd offered to mate her cursed. "She doesn't appear to be very sturdy."

"She's blooded enough to go into heat," Mark stated.

"It's very faint," the whiner complained. "I can barely detect it over the horrible wolf stink."

"I know." Mark reached behind him and drew out what looked like a plastic eyeglasses case. "I grabbed this on the way here."

"That will do it," the oldest-looking male said. "Those hormones will jumpstart her into full-blown heat. It takes about twenty minutes to work from the testing I've done."

"Hormones will do that?" The whiner didn't look convinced.

"They were taken straight from other she-cats in full heat. We've tested it a few times and it's worked every time."

"What are the chances of her dying?" Mark coldly glanced at Shannon. "I'd hate to take that risk. She's partially in heat already."

"The hormones won't kill her," the older male proclaimed. "We're just going to have to remember to be careful. She's going to suffer, but no biting or clawing her up. Blood loss *will* kill her."

Shannon started to tremble. "What are you talking about? What do you plan to do to me?"

Mark's green eyes fixed on her and he sighed. "What do you know of us?"

"You plan to kill me for being mostly human."

"Wrong." He walked closer. "Here's a little sex education for you. In skin, when we get females pregnant, they only have single births. One baby."

Dread filled Shannon. They were talking about sex, hormones, and her being in heat. She had a really bad feeling where this conversation was headed.

"But we can impregnate females with litters if we're shifted when it happens. They can carry anywhere from three to five

218

babies. The thing is, though, when the female shifts back to skin it aborts the pregnancy. Our women don't enjoy staying in animal form for months while their pregnancies gestate to full term. Even the ones willing to attempt it have accidentally shifted while they slept, without meaning to. It has greatly decreased our numbers. After we decided it was safer to mostly live in skin than remain in animal form, our low live-birth rate has greatly decreased our population."

Adam snorted. "Humans try to shoot us or give us to zoos when we run around shifted."

One of the men nodded. "I lost my first mate after humans killed her. Some fucking hunter shot her on private property. I killed him but she didn't survive his bullet. They poach on our lands after hearing about sightings of us. Now we can only shift and run at night to avoid drawing more of them. We post guards to take out any trespassers. They're easy to sneak up on using our night vision."

Mark took over the conversation again. "We can breed with *you* and create a litter. You can carry more babies than our females can."

Shannon whimpered. "I can't shift, and I won't do that. No!" Her frightened gaze darted among the seven men. She knew all the color drained from her face when she realized one of them planned to try to get her pregnant, and she pulled frantically at whatever held her wrists. "I won't agree to it!"

The oldest guy drew her attention by walking closer to peer down at her. "We're not asking your permission. You're not pride and your wishes are irrelevant. The fact that you can't shift is why you're perfect for what we need." He glanced at Mark. "Should you tell her or should I?"

"I will." Mark's green eyes seemed to gleam, his look of near amusement directed at Shannon. "Here's how it is. You can't shift, which means you can't accidentally abort the litter you'll carry."

She recoiled in revulsion. "But you said in skin, I'd only have one baby."

"*You'll* be in skin—but we won't." A cold smile curved Mark's lips. "We're going to shift after our doctor there injects you with hormones to force you into full heat, your body will be primed to conceive, and between all of us, we'll put a litter inside you."

Adam rubbed his hands together. "It's going to feel great for us but...not for you. That's why no male will fuck his mate the way we're going to take you, and we don't share our mates. Females are able to carry different babies from different fathers at the same time. Between the seven us, we'll definitely make sure you have a litter. Human and puma bodies just don't match up that well." He smiled at the men around him. "We've all fantasized about it though."

The doctor chuckled. "I've done it once to test the hormones. It's amazing. They're much wetter in skin so you can fuck them deeper, but we should gag her. She'll scream. It's very painful for the female when we barb up and withdraw from her. We can't wait

220

until we soften to pull out after ejaculation, the way we do with our mates. We need to keep fucking her continuously because the hormones won't last more than a few hours. It's too risky to keep her in heat with her human blood for longer than that. Her heart probably couldn't take the strain."

Shannon wanted to scream then. She resisted the urge as she fought her restraints and tried to get to her feet, but with her arms behind her back, she couldn't.

"Please don't do this," she begged.

Mark tossed the plastic case to the doctor. "Inject her. We'll prepare her while it starts to take effect. I'm not worried about her screaming. No one will hear her and we've posted a few guards."

The doctor caught the case, opened it, and withdrew a large syringe. Shannon threw her body to the side, tried to roll away, but he planted his loafer on her ass, pinned her to the ground, and tore up her shirt. Another male bent down to tear at the borrowed sweatpants she wore. He bared her left ass cheek.

Shannon screamed when the big needle pierced her skin. It hurt a lot and seemed to take a long time for the doctor to inject the contents. Tears ran down her face when she stopped screaming after the needle jerked out of her ass. Two men gripped her upper arms to haul her painfully off the ground. They didn't even let her feet touch the grass when they carried her toward a large fallen tree. Two other men rushed forward to help.

221

She screamed and struggled but they forced her to her knees and bent her over the rough wood. Someone cut the restraints at her wrists but then her arms were yanked wide apart. She turned her head to see rope being tied to branches still attached to the log, and then secured to her wrists to keep her arms spread open.

"Don't do this! Oh god. Please!" she sobbed.

"Shut up." Mark leapt over the log to face her from the other side. He picked up something that had been hidden from her view under the log—a chain with a thick leather collar. She tried to jerk away but the ropes held her firmly against the log. "This is to keep you in place. The less you fight, the less the risk of slicing you with our claws."

She tossed her head, tried to avoid his hands, but he managed to clamp the collar around her neck. It nearly choked her until he adjusted it. He bent, pulled on the chain, and it forced her head down until her chin brushed the log. She heard a click and when she tried to lift her head, there wasn't any give. Mark winked at her.

"I'm going first. You won't be able to see which one of you is fucking you since you can't turn your head but I wanted you to know that. Don't worry though. I'm the biggest so I'll hurt the most. The others will feel slightly less painful afterward. Strip her."

"I'm under the protection of a werewolf," she cried out when someone gripped the back of her shirt, jerking her body painfully, and material tore open to bare her skin. "He will kill you for doing this to me!"

222

Mark brushed his fingertips over her cheek. She tried to jerk away but the collar choked her. It made him laugh but he pulled his hand away.

"No werewolf is going to come after a she-cat. A dog will fuck anything, and I'm sure it was fun for him to screw the enemy in a literal sense. Now you're home. This is your life from now on. You'll breed us litters until you grow too old to have them anymore. You'll be useless when you stop ovulating but if you help hike our numbers high enough, we won't turn killing you into a fun sport. I'll make it painless." He winked again. "I'm a nice guy when motivated. Don't forget that."

She sobbed, the action making her more aware of the rough bark through the thin material of her shirt. They bared her back and tore the sweats off her completely. She screamed when her thighs were pulled apart, spread wide, and ropes were wrapped painfully into her legs just above her knees so she couldn't close them.

"Don't do that," Mark crooned. "You don't look as pretty with red eyes. Of course, I won't be looking at your face." He stood and moved out of her sight.

She could hear them talking while she cried. Her body started to feel warm, then hot, as if she were running a fever. Painful cramps jolted through her belly and she sobbed when the agony increased. Wetness slipped down her thighs, coated them. She knew she hadn't peed herself — the drugs were working.

"Fuck," someone snarled. "Smell her. Let's start."

223

"Not yet," the doctor ordered. "Soon. We want her in full ovulation. Let's strip and change. What's the order? We don't want us fighting to determine whose turn it is."

"I go first." Mark sounded as if he stood very close behind her. "Adam is next. The rest of you can decide the order. We're all going to have her, so don't snipe. We have hours with her. Whatever order you choose, keep it going. I figure we'll each get her three times at least."

Shannon screamed again. The raw sound tore through the woods but she knew no help would come. They were going to shift into animals to gang rape her.

Chapter Thirteen

This can't be happening. Shannon latched on to that thought with desperation. *They can't do this to me. It's not real. I'm having a nightmare. Wake up! Oh god, wake up!*

A high-pitched, animalistic scream distracted her from the prayer she had started to mentally chant. She had no idea what had caused the startling noise.

"What the hell?" Mark moved within sight in front of the log, glowering at the woods. "Was that one of ours?"

"Shit," Adam hissed. "I think word is out and we're about to have more company. I told all of you not to share news of her with anyone. Who did you tell?"

"No one," the whiner answered.

"I didn't," someone else protested.

Mark turned and rage twisted his features in an ugly expression. "Damn it, you were the only ones we could trust not to tear her apart. If half the pride shows up to take turns with her she won't survive."

Another strange scream tore through the woods. It seemed to come from a different direction...or maybe not. It was difficult for Shannon to distinguish.

"They seem to be fighting already." Mark muttered a string of curses as he walked out of her sight. "I'm going to have to challenge some of them now. I'll tear out your throats if one of you mounts her while I'm dealing with the approaching males. Got me? I get her first. If some of them get around me, you make sure they don't get to her. I'll have all your asses if I'm not the first. I want to make sure at least one in the litter she'll carry is mine."

The nightmare just grew worse for Shannon. Not only were seven of them planning to rape her, but now more of their pride seemed to want to join the torture. A new hell set in as her body further betrayed her. She could feel her sex swelling and her clit started to throb as though it had a heartbeat. The sensation grew painful and a new noise came from her mouth that she couldn't hold back, a throaty cry.

"She's in full heat," the doctor informed the group. "Look at her vulva. Pink and puffy and soaked. She's ready to conceive."

"Damn it!" Mark roared, obviously in a full-blown rage now. "Who the hell told our males about this?"

He leapt over the log into Shannon's view again. The sight of his naked backside jolted terror through her. He'd been ready to shift and take her body. She struggled but couldn't break free. Her gaze remained on Mark since, as long as he kept in front of her, she knew no one would touch her. He scanned the woods and then his body started to shift while he dropped to all fours.

"Fuck!" he roared. "Prepare to fight." His voice transformed from human to the scream of his animal.

She gaped at the sight of his sleek animal body. He was terrifying. She'd been to zoos before but the large cats there didn't seem as big to her as he did at that moment. Of course, they had been at a distance, not six feet away. She watched his ears pin back, his body tense, and he crouched.

Something rustled in the bushes and her gaze jerked toward the noise.

It wasn't another puma that ran into the clearing. A big wolf barreled directly at Mark. Three more large wolves exploded into the clearing from different angles.

The first wolf slammed into Mark.

All hell broke loose. The wolves attacked the shifting men. Adam jumped over the log to try to help his brother, tried to shift, but another big wolf tackled him, took his body down, and he screamed as sharp teeth tore at him. Blood flew, splattering the ground. Behind her, she heard more fighting and snarls. Something splattered her bare foot, a warm, wet sensation that she guessed was blood.

She couldn't see what happened behind her but she couldn't miss the fights in front of her between Mark in puma form and the big black wolf that had rushed out of the woods first. Mark swiped at the wolf but missed when it spun out of reach with mere inches to spare.

The wolf charged, head lowered, and slammed into the puma with enough force to knock it into the grass. The black wolf clamped his big jaws into the equally large cat's hind leg, shredding it. The cat screamed and tried to roll away.

One of them has to be Anton! she realized. *At least I hope so.* She wanted to yell his name as her gaze darted between the two wolves attacking Mark and Adam. The wolf holding Adam on the ground won his bloody victory. Adam stopped fighting. A mat of thick hair coated his arms, and his ears extended longer than a human's, but otherwise he appeared human. Bright red soaked his still form and she didn't see his chest moving.

The wolf who had killed him turned his head to stare at her with dark eyes.

"Anton?" Her voice shook.

He suddenly lunged forward but didn't stop in front of her. Instead, he snarled and jumped the log. He missed her by inches as he launched through the air. In seconds, something large, heavy, and hairy slammed against the back of her thighs.

She opened her mouth to scream but a snarl stopped her cold. It sounded more like a dog than anything. A vicious, pissed-off wolf. It pushed away from her and she heard a loud shriek, and more wetness splashed her leg. Then something hairy and thin slapped the back of her thigh. It did it again. She tried to turn her head but the collar prevented it. A few more swats and she realized it had to be a tail wagging against her.

What the hell? Is that Anton trying to comfort me with his tail? Trying to let me know he's there protecting my back?

She focused on the fight in front of her. The cat and wolf still fought but the cat bled a lot. It tried to run away but the wolf took it down from behind, landing on it and lunging for the throat. The cat screamed and then thrashed under the powerful jaws gripping it, the wolf's head shaking back and forth to cause more injury.

Mark stilled under the wolf forever.

The wolf released the dead carcass and turned. He met Shannon's gaze and slowly inched closer. His head was tucked down a little, his jaws dripped blood but were closed now. He advanced until he stood mere feet from her. He collapsed and started to transform into skin.

His side had been mauled by the cat's claws. Red, bloody marks marred tan skin. He had more cuts and a bite on his thigh. She gasped when she realized who it was as he lifted his head.

Anton's brother, Rave, met her gaze and gave her a wink. "I'll be okay. I'll be healed from this in a matter of days."

The sounds of fighting ceased behind her and the tail stopped tapping her thigh. She gasped when something cold and wet suddenly nudged against her swollen pussy. She tried to fight when it pressed tighter, until it slid along the folds of her sex and she heard sniffing. She hated the way her body responded. Pleasure rolled through her at just the brush of something against her clit and she fought the urge to come that fast.

Rave lifted his large body up and gripped the log to peer over the other side. He growled. "Anton, what the hell are you doing?"

The cold, wet nose jerked away from her body and she relaxed, knowing it had been Anton touching her intimately. His brother lowered his face level with her and met her gaze. She avoided glancing at his groin. The guy wasn't wearing anything but blood on his skin. His fingers gripped the collar.

"Sorry. My brother just wanted to make sure none of those pride males raped you. I'll assume they didn't since he's not going nuts." He cocked his head to peer behind her. "He's changing back now. Give him a minute to get back into skin. Let's get this collar off you."

His touch made her hurt worse. She squeezed her eyes closed and took shallow breaths. Desire shot through her to the point that she had to clench her teeth not to moan at just the brush of his fingers pressed between her throat and the leather to unfasten it. The heavy weight dropped away and new hands gripped her hips. She started, her eyes flying open.

"It's Anton." Rave frowned at her, sniffed, and then paled. "Fuck." He fell on his ass to get away from her.

230

"What did they do to you?" Anton's voice scared her. He snarled when he spoke.

She turned her head now that she could. Rage gripped his features—his fangs still out, and deadly. Blood was smeared all over his body. The hold on her hips tightened.

"They turned you on?" He started to breathe faster—panting—and his eyes shifted enough to wolf. "Are you sorry I showed up? Did I interrupt a party?"

Shock and hurt lanced through her. Her lips parted but nothing came out.

"Damn it, Anton," a man snarled. "Does she look willing? They have her tied down. See the ropes? Move!"

A stranger grabbed Anton's shoulder and pushed him aside. Shannon realized the guy had to be related, with his black hair and similar features. His eyes were more of a light brown though. He hesitated.

"It's okay. I'm Brand Harris. I'm their cousin. I'm going to get you free. He doesn't understand what's happened to you. I'll try like hell to avoid touching your skin. I know you've got to be hurting pretty bad and touch makes it worse." His nose flared and he softly groaned. "You're in full heat."

Anton suddenly lunged, almost stepped on Shannon's leg to put his body between her and his cousin. "Don't touch Shannon!

231

Think I don't see how you react to her? Jesus. That's my woman you're sporting wood over!"

"Damn it, Anton! I'm not going to mount her. I'm just reacting. I've got a pulse. She's in the most intense stage of heat. I told you I used to live with one of her kind. It's not her fault that she's aroused this strongly. It's got nothing to do with what they planned to do to her. It's biology. She can't help what her body is doing. Any touch is going to be hell. Just untie her if you won't let me do it. She's going to be super sensitive at the slightest…hell. You don't know anything about what she's going through, do you?"

"No," Anton growled. "I know you want to fuck her."

"I can't help reacting to her scent."

Someone cleared his throat. "If you need any help tending to her, Anton, I'm offering. Damn, she's affecting me too. I thought *our* women smelled good."

Anton spun to glare at Rave. "You touch her and I'll kill you," he snarled. "And fuck you for getting a boner. She's *mine*."

"She won't be if we don't get the hell out of here," one of the others argued. "I'm sporting wood too. Don't yell at me. It's a physical reaction, Anton. We aren't going to try to mount her. We need to leave before the two who escaped return with reinforcements. I'm sure you'd rather fuck her than fight off more who want to take her from you."

Anton's hands worked the ropes free. She clenched her teeth not to moan when his fingers brushed her skin. She refused to look at him, humiliated by her body's reaction, the discussion she'd listened to, and the fact that it seemed that every male in Anton's family had an erection over her scent. They'd also seen her naked and spread-eagle.

When he freed her legs, she clamped her thighs together and clutched the torn shirt over her breasts. She wanted to curl into a ball, hide her body as best she could, and cry. The pain staggered her now — sharp stabs of fire — and she couldn't manage to get to her feet.

"Shannon?" Anton's voice softened. "Look at me."

She refused. She focused on the ground instead. He softly cursed and his hands gripped her hips. The touch made her cry out and she threw herself forward and hit the log hard enough to scrap her skin. She huddled against it.

"You're such a jerk," Brand muttered. "They were going to rape her and you think she wanted it just because her body is in heat. Move out of the way and I'll carry her."

"You touch her and I'll tear your head off!" Anton threatened with a snarl.

Someone crouched behind her close enough that she could smell him. It made her whimper. Her body burned and her breasts

233

tightened until her nipples throbbed. She pressed tighter against the log, the rough bark better than having one of them touching her.

"I'm sorry," Anton rasped softly. "I was out of my head, okay? Rave told me what they do to unmated half-breed females, how they use them to carry their young, and I didn't think I'd reach you in time. I know that you didn't want them. I'm going to pick you up. We have a van about a mile from here. We need to get you back to pack territory before more of those pride males show up. I can protect you better there."

"I'll walk," she whispered.

"Damn," he ground out harshly. "You aren't in any condition to walk. Don't fight me."

He jerked her away from the log and scooped her up in his arms. Her back arched and she hissed. His warm body drew her, though, and she turned into him, pressed tightly against him, and buried her face against his skin. His masculine scent made her moan and twist within his hold. Her hands gripped his shoulder and chest, her fingers kneading his skin frantically.

"We need to go," he muttered. "Let's hurry. If I see anyone staring at her body, it will be the last thing you ever look at."

The jarring motion of him jogging with her cradled against his body made her writhe in his arms. Sexual desire fogged her brain. She made soft crying sounds she couldn't stop from passing her lips and sometimes a rumble would vibrate in her chest. It was almost a whining. She hated being out of control, and the fact that there were witnesses made it worse.

"Get the door," Anton ordered. "Brand, you drive to stay as far from her as you can get."

"I'm not going to try to fuck her!" the cousin snapped. "It's just physical. You're aroused too. We all are."

He nearly crushed her when he ducked down to move inside the van. He gently placed her on a cool leather seat and then dropped down next to her. She turned away from him toward the window, huddled on the seat with her knees drawn up, and kept her back to him. She sat on the back bench seat of an extended travel van with tinted windows. The other guys climbed inside and the van doors slammed closed.

"We'll dress later," someone announced. "I know I can't put my jeans on in this state. My zipper might catch skin even if I *could* shove my dick inside enough to attempt to get them closed. Roll down the windows, Brand. Turn on the air conditioning too. Now I can taste her. Why the hell didn't anyone ever tell me that's how they smelled in heat? I would have hooked up with one long ago."

Anton snarled. "Silence, Braden. Someone toss me a shirt to cover her with. She's trembling."

The van engine started and the vehicle rolled forward. Shannon slid into a big, warm Anton when Brand made a sharp U-turn on the narrow two-lane road. Just brushing up against Anton made her hotter. She fought the urge to stay there. She tried to pull away but then he wrapped an arm around her waist to secure her at his side.

"Here's a shirt. Let's put this on you."

She moaned. The heavy weight of his arm just under her breasts made her arch and her hand gripped his bare leg, rubbed it frantically, and then clutched his inner thigh. Anton groaned in response, yanked his arm from her, and shoved the shirt over her head to pull it down her body.

"Damn," Anton rasped. "You're on fire, aren't you, kitten?"

She nodded and tears filled her eyes. She wanted him now, needed him, and knew if she followed her instincts, she'd beg him to take her inside a van with his family watching. She'd never recover from the horror of it. She wasn't the type. She'd known women who had sex in public and hadn't ever understood why they'd do something that awful. She'd never been in heat before though.

She turned her head and met his concerned gaze. "Not in front of them. Please? Don't let me. I—" She choked on a sob. "Please?"

Anton had never felt so helpless in his entire life—or like such a complete asshole. He'd screwed up big time when he'd accused her of wanting to be fucked by the pride males who'd kidnapped her. He'd been shocked and then enraged when he'd realized how sexually excited she'd been while tied to that log. Seeing her restrained and her body displayed, totally exposed to all the males who'd stared at her pussy, had sent him into a jealous rage.

He knew mating heat affected his kind, made a male mindless to fuck at times, but it seemed cats ended up with a worse deal. A female werewolf would only want the male who'd marked her. She'd fight to the death if another male tried to mount her. The touch of another male wouldn't feel good. It would grate on her nerves to the point of pain. Shannon wasn't a werewolf.

The hand on his leg tightened and tears spilled down her face. It assured him of the hellish situation she experienced. He could smell her lust, see the desperation in her gaze, and understood what she'd tried to say to him. She was losing control, the heat overtaking her ability to think, but she would be mortified later if he took her in front of others.

"As soon as we hit our territory, pull over," Anton demanded loudly. "How far?"

"Ten miles." Brand cursed. "Is she going to make it? Charma, the human, half spotted leopard I dated, used to just about lose her mind. If she even started to scent of going into heat, I'd stay home with her. I was always terrified she'd go into heat when I wasn't there. It would get so bad that she probably would have attacked any male she came into contact with. The mailman would have been in for a hell of a surprise. I would have murdered the bastard if that ever happened."

237

Shannon cried more, a look of pure horror on her features at hearing that news. It pissed him off.

"Shut up, Brand."

"Sorry." The engine grew louder when he punched the gas. "I'm breaking every speed limit."

Anton groaned when Shannon leaned into him, rubbing up against his chest, and his dick turned to stone. The smell of her drove his mating heat into full-blown lust. He wanted to shove her flat on the seat and drive into her, balls deep. His hands gripped her hips, locking her into place where she sat, and then she started to purr. She nipped at his chest with her teeth. It sent a jolt straight to his cock.

Rave turned his head to gawk at Anton. "The sound of her purring is really sexy."

"Turn around, damn it. How are we doing, Brand?" He glared at his brother until he followed his order.

"I'm doing seventy. It would be really bad if a cop pulled us over. I doubt he'd understand why five guys are naked with a chick who's in her condition."

"Just take her," Von urged, turning in his seat. "How can you not? I want to climb back there and do her if you won't. It's torture hearing her agony."

Anton made a vicious sound. "Turn around!"

238

Von muttered an oath but faced the front. Anton watched his brothers to make sure they didn't glance at Shannon and tried to fight the urge to fuck her, regardless of where they were. He knew it would make her hate him. He needed to be strong for both of them. That became more difficult when she clutched at his arms, kneading his skin and whimpering.

"Please," she begged. "It hurts so much."

"We're almost there. Just hold on to me."

She tried to move, her intention to straddle him clear, and he snarled at her. He hoped her instincts would make fear override her lust. Her head jerked up to peer at him, her lovely eyes filled with such pain that he felt like an even bigger bastard.

"Almost there. Just a few more minutes."

She lowered her face and pressed it back against his chest. Her teeth and tongue tormented him as she spread desperate, wet kisses over his skin. She purred louder, her entire body vibrating, and frantically stroked her body against his where they touched. His balls drew up tight and his cock pulsated painfully. If she kept it up, combined with her scent, he feared he'd embarrass himself by coming without ever entering her.

"Almost there," Brand promised again.

"Just pull off the road so no one can see the van and then take a hike. Guard us from a distance." He had to take a breath to calm down enough so they could understand his words. Talking became difficult. "Backs to the van. Understand me?"

"You don't want us watching." Von sighed. "Got it, bro. You're very protective of her."

"She's mine," Anton announced.

Braden turned in his seat. "You love her, don't you?"

Anton glared at him. "Now is not the time to discuss this."

"She's part cat. If our enforcers aren't in time to find and warn Dad, and Mom kills him, you're our new alpha. You can't mate her, Anton. It would tear the pack apart."

Von answered before Anton could. "Enough, Braden. That's secondary. If he loves her, we'll find a way to make it work for the pack. If they won't accept her then I'll step up to the plate, but you never ask a brother to give up a woman he loves."

"You don't want to lead the pack," Braden argued. "You always say it's a shit job and there isn't any reason you'd do it."

"That was before Anton fell for *her*." He blew out a deep breath. "I'll take the hit if he wants to mate her. His happiness is the most important thing."

"Thank you," Anton whispered.

Von glanced at him and then Shannon, then back at Anton. "I knew how you felt when you wanted us to declare war on a pride by going after her. There will be repercussions down the road. We killed some of their males."

"They stole her from me."

"Actually, Mom gave her to them," Rave stated. "I knew she could be cruel but this is beyond forgivable. She knew you'd marked your woman, realized the hell you'd suffer if you lost her, put your life in danger, but didn't give a damn. She put all of our lives at risk."

"We're here!" Brand yelled. "Hang on." He barely hit the brakes before they left the road.

Anton grabbed hold of Shannon tightly and the seat in front of him to keep them in place. Brand pulled far from the road, parked the van behind some trees, and killed the engine.

"We'll be guarding you from afar," Rave swore, meeting Anton's gaze. "We won't spy. As you said, she's yours. We respect that."

Rave shot a warning glare at the brothers as they bailed out of the van. He grabbed the men's pants out of their pile of clothes before the doors slammed shut. Anton watched them go until they moved out of sight. He turned to deal with Shannon.

"We're alone."

He pushed her onto her back on the bench seat, startled when she gasped, and his hands gripped her thighs. He salivated at the sight of her hot, swollen pussy dripping with her desire. He slid off the seat to his knees, cursed the tight fit between the seats as he shoved his ass against the back of the other bench seat and lowered his face.

"I'm dying too."

Chapter Fourteen

Shannon clawed at the back of the seat with one hand while gripping the edge of it at her side with the other, just to keep down when Anton suddenly shoved her onto her back. He spread her legs wide and, to help him, she lifted the leg against the seat to rest it along the top edge.

"I'm going to make it all better," he snarled a second before his tongue licked a wide path up her slit to her clit.

The contact made her cry out. Her entire pussy throbbed painfully. She threw her head back when his mouth fastened around her clit and he sucked. She came with a scream at just the sensation of it. The climax tore through her brutally but the pain remained.

Anton didn't stop. His tongue slid across the engorged bud over and over until she came again.

He released her clit and his tongue started to push inside her pussy. He snarled and jerked back. "You're so swollen I can't get in." He replaced a finger where his mouth had been, pressed against her, and she screamed when he wiggled inside her tight channel. He froze.

"Don't stop. I need you," she panted. "It feels good."

He worked his finger in deeper, filling the void that had her hurting the most, and she trembled. She needed more, faster, harder, but couldn't form words as he started to slowly slide his finger in and out of her. Her hips moved to arch against him. She had no control of her body and couldn't stop the noises coming from her, which normally would have frightened her. She growled and made mewling sounds.

He added another finger, stretched her, and she came again. The pleasure terrified her, the sensations too intense, but the need remained no matter how often he brought her to climax. Just pumping his fingers inside her wasn't enough. She needed more.

"Anton," she begged.

"I don't have condoms." His voice had turned scary deep, more of a snarl than words.

Her eyes opened and she stared at his face. He'd partially changed. His fangs were out, the shape of his eyes narrow, and he had more facial hair than normal but he still looked mostly human. Her hand released the side of the seat to grip his forearm.

"I need you."

"I know but I want you to understand what could happen. It's difficult for me to think, I'm in heat too, but I seem to have a tiny bit more control. I could mate you if I totally lose it or I could get you pregnant. I'm willing to risk both. I'd kill to be inside you."

"Please!" she urged.

His eye color bled to pure black and he withdrew his fingers from her pussy. He yanked her body down the seat a little and his arm slid under her back to help her sit up. She pressed back against the seat and he dragged her ass to the edge. Her gaze lowered down his chest to where he stood on his knees between her spread thighs. She stared at his cock.

He looked bigger than he ever had, the skin so red and swollen it appeared painful, and his cock twitched, the crown weeping fluid. Anton wrapped his hand around his shaft to guide it to her. She'd never watched a guy take her before but she couldn't look away as his other arm lifted her leg higher and wider to make room for his hips.

He pressed the tip of his cock against her pussy and then slowly entered her. She hissed at the pressure of something so thick penetrating her. The stretching sensation didn't hurt but it nearly made her come again. He wasn't even fully inside her yet. Anton rumbled deep within his chest—part moan, part growl.

"So hot and tight," he rasped. "Tell me if I hurt you."

His hand released his shaft and he grabbed her hip then slid his hand around to grip her ass. He drew closer, made her take more of his cock inside her, and Shannon clutched at his arms just for something to cling to. Ecstasy shot through her from the pressure of his rigid flesh and from the friction of him filling her.

"Look at me."

Her gaze lifted. She knew he barely kept a leash on his beast. She could see the wolf lurking in his dark gaze. She wondered if she looked as animalistic. The raw sex appeal of him barely keeping his humanity made her buck her hips, urging him on.

"Take me."

"Fuck," he snarled, and drove all the way inside her to the hilt.

Shannon growled, threw her head back, and her nails dug into his skin. Her hips wiggled frantically. "More. Again," she urged.

"I couldn't stop if I tried. You've got both sides of me, kitten."

He nearly withdrew from her fully and then he slammed back inside. His powerful body dominated hers. He fucked her forcefully and fast, deeply, and she gave herself up to sensation. She came and he roared out. His hips slowed a few thrusts and then he started again. It drove her passion on.

Sweat coated both their bodies, helping them glide together seamlessly. Time ceased to exist. At one point he withdrew from her, turned her over onto her knees, and pinned her body over the seat. She had to force her hands to let go of him to grip the back of the seat just for something to hold on to. He entered her from behind, drove into her frantically, and she screamed out as another climax gripped her just from the feel of the new position.

I'm not going to survive this, her mind sobbed. Anton powered in and out of her pussy, fucking her with an intensity that should have scared her, but she needed and wanted more. Another wave of pleasure overcame her, her throat sore from the sounds she made, but all that mattered was the ecstasy rolling throughout her body. Hands gripped her hips to hold her still as she tried to push back to keep urging him on.

"Shannon," he groaned. "Fuck." He roared out, slowed slightly, and the feel of his semen shooting inside her triggered another climax.

"More," she whispered.

His response was to start thrusting inside her again, this time slower, seeming to want to torture her. She gripped the seat and shoved back against his hands, slamming him inside her deeper, and she climaxed. Black spots twinkled as she stared at the seat in front of her face. A dizzy spell nearly overtook her but then Anton started to drive in and out of her strongly, moving fast, the way she wanted, and her need overrode her exhaustion.

Anton howled out when he came, his release triggering yet another orgasm inside her weary body, and this time she couldn't fight off the dizziness. She slumped against the seat, panted, and finally the pain eased. The need slowly faded.

"Shannon?" Alarm sounded in his voice.

"I'm okay," she got out. "Tired. It's not hurting anymore."

He leaned over her back, his hands tracing from her hips to her breasts to caress them, and he brushed a tender kiss on her shoulder.

"I'm going to take care of you. Rest, okay?"

She nodded and wanted to turn to snuggle against him but instead she closed her eyes, and Anton's soft curse was the last sound she heard.

Every muscle inside Anton's body ached. He'd gone through plenty of mating heats but none had been as exhausting or as pleasurable as the time he'd just spent with Shannon. He lifted her into his arms to adjust her sleeping form on the bench seat, careful not to trap her hair underneath her back when he laid her flat.

She looked pale to him and he wanted to curse a blue streak. She might be part shifter but he'd forgotten how human she was as well. He reached for the shirt he'd ripped off her during sex, realizing only then that he had, and spread it over her bared breasts. He turned his head, examined the van, and found the pile of clothing they'd left behind when they'd driven to pride lands, stripped, and transformed to hunt the males who'd taken Shannon. Only shirts and his pants remained.

He grabbed Rave's shirt to cover her from ribs to thighs. The overpowering smell of sex inside the van made him groan. His cock twitched and he grimaced at his stiffening member. "Stay down, damn it."

He grabbed his pants, opened the side door and pulled them on. Then he opened all the doors to air out the van and let out a low

248

whistle he knew his family would hear. Within minutes his brothers and cousin walked out of the woods from different directions.

"That was fast," Brand said.

"Fast?" Braden snorted. "I thought we'd have to camp out here tonight. It's been about three hours. The sun is about to go down."

"Shut up," Rave snapped. He gave Anton his full attention. "Is she okay?"

"She's asleep. She's not as strong as we are. She passed out cold from exhaustion."

Brand withdrew the keys from his front pocket. "She's going to be in heat for a few days. Feed her when she wakes, get as much rest as you can between bouts of sex, and don't leave her for anything. If you're there, she'll come after *you*. If you're not…" He paused. "It won't be her fault if the pain takes her reason and she goes after another male."

Rage surged through Anton at the idea of anyone else touching Shannon. "That won't ever happen."

Brand studied him. "I believe you. It used to be Charma's worst fear. It never happened to her but she'd heard stories of other females going nuts and waking up after some of the worst of the heat passed to find themselves with strangers. There are pills they can take to lessen the symptoms but I don't know how you'd get ahold of them. Charma'ld get horny but it was manageable for her. There are also pills cats have to prevent pregnancy."

249

Braden groaned. "Pregnant? Is that even possible? She's a puma and we're wolves."

Brand shrugged. "She's mostly human, and we know we can breed with *them*."

"That would be a nightmare," Braden muttered.

Rage simmered under Anton's skin and he took a threatening step toward his youngest brother. "Seal your mouth or eat my fist. If Shannon is pregnant, I'll be happy about it."

Rave threw his hand out and smacked the youngest brother on the back of the head. "Dumbass. That's your possible niece or nephew you just called a nightmare. You sound like our mother."

Braden flinched. "Sorry."

"Take us home. We need to find out if Dad is safe and I want Shannon to wake in my bed." Anton glanced at his family. "Thank you for helping me find her in time."

"We're brothers." Rave smiled. "I know you would be there if I needed you."

"You could have gone after Dad instead." Anton had worried about that.

Rave hesitated. "He knows how deceitful our mother can be at times. He defends her fucked-up actions. Your woman is an innocent in this, a victim, and there were other wolves to help Dad. It was a no-brainer for me."

"That's what we have enforcers for," Von reminded them. "To help us when we're busy. I'm just glad we found Shannon." He shot a curious look at Rave. "How did you know where they'd take her?"

"I told you. I go undercover to hang out at the biker bar that borders their lands. I hear shit about the pride. We have a meeting tree in our woods, and they have a log." He shrugged. "I figured that would be the most logical place for them to take her. I'm just glad they were so predictable. Otherwise we would have had to grab one of their members, torture them into telling us the location, and we might have been too late."

"I owe all of you," Anton promised softly.

"Want me to smack *you* on the back of the head next for being a dumbass?" Rave grinned. "Shut up. The only thing I'm pissed about is the fact I'm in heat and you'll kill me if I touch the only woman within a mile of us. Let's go. I have a woman at my place who's probably pretty pissed she's had to wait for me."

Anton climbed back inside the van and sat on the bench seat in front of Shannon. Her breathing was slow and steady. He met Rave's gaze when he slumped into the seat in front of him.

"She's beautiful, bro. And I can see the way you look at her. Don't allow politics to screw up your happiness."

251

"I meant it when I offered," Von interrupted. "I don't want to lead the pack but if you mate her and the others won't follow you because of it, I'll step up to the plate. Your happiness comes first."

Emotion nearly overwhelmed Anton. "Thank you."

Von shrugged. "It's not as though I have a life. Besides, I can't see our father stepping down anytime soon. He's strong and healthy. He could hold the pack for decades." He paused. "Did you mate her? I don't smell blood but it would be too soon to scent a change in both of you if you had."

"I can't smell anything but sex," Braden grumbled. "This is mean, by the way. I'm in heat too. I think my dick is permanently bent at an odd angle from wearing pants in this condition. I'm sorry I grabbed them when we headed off into the woods."

Rave snorted. "I heard your heavy breathing. You didn't keep the pants on the entire time." He winked. "Is your hand tired or did you switch up?"

"Shut up." Braden blushed. "I could hear them. Don't tell me I was the only one."

"It's all about control." Von snickered. "We all have women waiting for us. I wasn't jacking off. I prefer the real thing."

Brand started the van and backed out of the woods, onto the road. He threw it in drive and punched the gas. "Don't let them get to you, Braden. I don't have a woman waiting for me and you weren't alone." He turned his head and smiled. "I switched up. It

252

helps keep my biceps even so one arm isn't bigger than the other. Remember that." He returned his focus to the road.

"Fuck," Anton groaned. "I'm glad Shannon is sleeping. She gets embarrassed easily. I never want any of you to mention this. Let her think you couldn't hear anything and nobody got off with us." He glared at Braden. "You better have been picturing another woman in your fantasies."

His brother blushed again.

Anton snarled and lunged. Rave grabbed him and shoved him back against his seat.

"Don't. He's a kid."

"I'm twenty-five," Braden protested. "I'm fully grown."

"But you're not overly bright to think about your brother's woman while you're jacking off." Von chuckled. "At least learn to lie."

Rave laughed and only released Anton after he relaxed back against his seat. "Dumbass."

"Fuck you," Braden growled.

"Seems you do fine on your own," Rave shot back.

"Just get us home." Anton turned his head to watch Shannon. "And slow down, Brand. I don't want the rough road to wake her."

He ignored his brothers, his sole focus on the sleeping woman.

A cell phone rang. Von twisted his body and yanked it from his back pocket.

"Von here." He listened for a while. "Thanks."

"Well? Was that news from our enforcers?"

"That was Dad. The enforcers found him with Mother, having sex. When he would talk to them and got past his anger at them interrupting, he wasn't pleased with what they had to say. He wants us at the house *now*."

"Drop me off at my place," Anton ordered. "Shannon is my priority."

Von hesitated. "It's a direct order. He wants us all there."

"I don't care."

"Anton, don't do this. Dad is upset. You should have heard him. You're his son, probably his favorite since he's been training you since birth to take his place, and he just found out his mate betrayed you both. He needs you. You can bring her with us. I heard Brand about not letting her out of your sight. If she gets bad again, you can take her to your old room at the house. We all understand mating heat."

"Okay. Stop at my place first though. I want her in clothes when we go to our parents' house. Did he mention if any of the pack is there?"

"He didn't." Von shoved his phone back into his pocket. "Brand, you heard him. Stop at the bar first."

"Got it." Brand sighed. "Remember when the biggest problem we had used to be remembering to carry enough condoms at this

254

time of year? Things were less complicated when we were younger."

Anton gazed at Shannon's face. "I wouldn't go back for anything. I've found what I've been looking for all my life."

"Shit." Braden groaned. "He's going to mate her. Great. A cat in the family. I can just imagine the pussy jokes the guys are going to torment me with now."

Anton smiled when he heard the sound of a hand slap the back of Braden's head and his responding curse. Rave had nailed him again. Some things never changed.

Chapter Fifteen

Shannon awoke when Anton forced her into a shower with him. The pain she'd suffered from going into heat had faded to a dull ache. Her muscles were sore but the shower helped. Anton tended her by washing her hair and body with his big, gentle hands.

"We have to go to my parents' house. I'm sorry I had to wake you. My family is outside waiting for us." He turned off the water after quickly washing his hair. "How are you feeling?"

Her cheek remained a little tender from being hit by Mark. She could still feel the heat there, but didn't mention it hurt. Anton had been injured far worse with his gashes and bruises when he'd fought to rescue her. She didn't want to complain about something trivial in comparison.

"Sore but more like myself."

"According to my cousin, who seems to know a lot about your kind, this could last for days. If you start to hurt, tell me immediately. Do you need me?"

"I'm a little turned on. You're hard. I noticed but I'm okay. There's no pain. I'll wait here while you go to your parents' house."

He shoved a towel at her. "No. I'm not leaving you alone."

Fear sprang forth. "You think those jerks will come after me again?"

He hesitated. "I don't want your heat to return while I'm not here to take care of you."

Memory surfaced of something his cousin had said and she stared at the floor. "Oh. You think I'll hit on someone." Mortification gripped her. "I'll go with you."

A hand gripped her chin, forced it up, and she met his intense gaze. "I didn't mean what I said in the woods. I was jealous and worried they'd hurt you. I told you, when I shift I'm more wolf than...me. I know you didn't want them to fuck you. My wolf was going nuts."

Tears filled her eyes. "I've never even had a one-night stand. Is it really possible that I'd allow anyone to touch me while I'm in heat?"

"I don't know. We're never going to find out, either. No male will ever get near you when you're vulnerable. It's just going to be me."

Her mouth parted but she held back the words.

"What?"

She licked her lips. "What about the next time? You won't be with me then. I mean, if I'm similar to a cat, this will return if those hormones they gave me triggered me to change more, or woke dormant genes."

He tensed. "Hormones?"

"They gave me a shot to force me into heat. I'm hoping now that they've probably dissipated in my system that it will never be that bad again. It could have just been from what they did to me when they gave me that shot. I really hope that's the case. I never want to go through that again. It hurt so much, being in full heat. I'm not sure I could take suffering that kind of agony again."

"We'll discuss this later. We need to get dressed and go to my parents' house."

She glanced down at his cock. "You're aroused."

"You're naked and I'm in mating heat. This is how I'm going to stay. I can control myself for a while. I can make it a few hours without the need growing too strong. We'll be home by then."

Shannon dropped the towel and eased to her knees to kneel on it in front of him. Anton had to release her face when she did it. She saw his eyes widen with surprise as she licked her lips.

"You took care of me. Now it's my turn to take care of you."

His cock stiffened more, lifted straight up, and desire made him growl softly at her. "They're waiting for us." He paused. "But I'm not saying no." A grin transformed his lips. "Learning patience won't hurt them."

She hesitated and then her hand brushed his thigh, caressed his skin, and her fingers brushed his shaft. For someone so hard, the texture of his skin felt velvety soft.

"I don't have much experience at this."

He brushed her hair back over her shoulder. "Open up and take me. You couldn't do it wrong. I'd enjoy anything you do to me."

Her lips parted and he leaned closer. She adjusted him until the crown of his cock hovered just over her bottom lip. Her tongue slipped out to swirl around the rim. A soft groan came from Anton. It encouraged her to grow bolder when she opened her mouth to make room for his thick size. She pressed forward, taking him inside, and sealed her lips around him.

She remembered the basics though it had been years since she'd given a guy head. She hadn't enjoyed it the few times she'd tried. Her ex-boyfriend had always choked her by grabbing the back of her head to try to make her take more than she could handle. Anton didn't do that. He had her hair but he just held it out of the way. His hips didn't thrust forward. He held very still.

"Go slow," he urged.

She started to move around him, lightly sucking and licking at him. His cock seemed to grow stiffer and his breathing increased but he held still. She took more of him, feeling more secure that she could handle his girth. A taste filled her mouth, a wonderful masculine flavor, and she moaned, moving faster, wanting more. It surprised her and her body responded. Her nipples grew taut and she started to ache for sex. Wetness began to spread down her inner thighs.

"Fuck," Anton moaned. "Slow down, Shannon. I can't come inside your mouth. I'm afraid I'd make you choke. We tend to ejaculate harder and longer while in heat."

She wanted to taste him enough to take that risk and ignored his warning. She moved faster, took him deeper, and sucked with gusto. Anton suddenly gripped her jaw, his hand tightening on her hair, and jerked back. His cock pulled free from her hungry mouth and she cried out. She stared at him with confusion.

He fell to his knees in front of her, grabbed her around her waist, and lifted her easily to turn her around. "Bend and grab the edge of the sink now," he snarled.

Her hands clutched porcelain and she cried out when he entered her fast and hard from behind. His cock stretched her, sent rapture straight to her brain from the nerve endings he pressed against as he surged into her deeply, his hands steadying her hips.

"Hang on tight," he rasped.

He pounded against her ass, fucking her furiously, and the sounds of their panting and skin slapping skin filled the small room. Shannon hung her head, pleasure swamping her, and her vaginal muscles tightened in anticipation of the climax that built. No one had ever made her feel the way Anton could.

Anton's hands moved. One released her hip to grip her shoulder while his other hand delved between her parted thighs. Two fingers pressed against her clit. He rubbed her while he fucked her. Shannon screamed when she started to come. The world exploded around her in ecstasy. A heavy body pressed against her back and teeth gripped her shoulder on the side he wasn't holding. His teeth pinched her skin, sent more rapture throughout her body, and he snarled.

His teeth pulled away and then he roared loud enough in her ear to deafen her while his body jerked violently. Inside, she could feel him filling her with his release. Each jerk of his hips spilled more of his cum inside her. The warm jets of his semen spread and it made her smile at the rightfulness of the sensation.

"Fuck," he groaned. "I nearly did it. We have to talk after we get back from my parents'."

She turned her head to stare into his beautiful eyes. "You were going to mate me, weren't you? We didn't use a condom."

He didn't look away. Their faces nearly touched with him bent over her, their bodies still joined, and his fingers eased away from her throbbing clit. "Yes. I wanted to mate you, and I'm aware that we didn't use one this time when we could have."

She didn't know what to say. Disappointment that he hadn't bitten her wasn't something she wanted to share. Staying with Anton, despite the fact they didn't know each other well, wouldn't be a bad thing. She was falling in love with him. She kept that bit of news a secret as well, sure he would do the normal guy thing when he heard a woman say the "L word"—run.

261

It's just sex, she told herself. *He made a commitment to me during mating heat. When it's over, he's going to want me gone. He's a werewolf and I'm not. He's the future alpha of his pack and I can't forget that.*

"We need to shower again and then go." He hesitated and then a look of regret crossed his features. "We'll talk when we return." He lifted up and carefully withdrew from her body.

She hated it when their bodies were no longer connected. She loved feeling a part of Anton. She just loved *him*. He'd saved her from his pack, from a puma pride, and he always took care of her. In other words, he'd done more for her than any other guy ever had. He made her feel safe and protected. Special. Sexy. All the things she'd always longed to feel. He also knew she wasn't fully human, accepted her despite it, and had given her amazing, mind-blowing sex. A lot of it too.

Anton stood and held out his hands. "Come on."

She allowed him to pull her to her feet. He released her, turned the water back on, and stepped inside the shower. She hesitated. *When we come back here, will he tell me that we could never work out, long term? Remind me that a cat and a wolf can never be anything more than temporary lovers?* It hurt her to even consider those possibilities.

"Come on in. The water is warm." He smiled at her.

Her heart melted even more. She stepped into the shower with him and allowed the water to flow over her body. In minutes they got out, dried off, and Anton lent her a pair of sweatpants and one of his oversized T-shirts.

262

"It's going to be fine," he assured her, his dark gaze holding hers. "You know you're safe with me, and I'll never allow anyone to hurt you. I don't know how many of our pack may be there but my mother will be for sure. She won't get near you."

"Okay." She believed him. "I know she hates me after the scene she made when she visited earlier. Is your father okay?"

"We need to go. My father wasn't hurt. My mother lied about that to lure me away from you. She's the reason those pride males knew where to find you." He grimaced. "She called them to come get you. It's fine now. My father will handle this and make certain it never happens again. She's in deep shit right now with everyone. I need to speak to him and he's waiting for us."

She nodded, lifted her chin, and gave him a brave face. He led her out of the apartment, down the stairs, and they left the closed bar by the back door. They didn't speak, though she had questions.

The white van waited outside with his brothers and cousin. She refused to meet their gazes. It made her embarrassed that these men knew she and Anton had sex in the same van she climbed into again. She also wondered how Anton had gotten her from the van up to his apartment. Okay, she really didn't want to know, for fear the answer would make her more uncomfortable, but she hoped he'd covered up her body somehow instead of carrying her naked in front of his family. Witnessing her tied naked to that log had been bad enough.

Anton sat next to her and took her hand in his. She clung to him as the van started. Meeting his mother had been an unpleasant experience and now she would meet his father. Alphas were the most feared of all werewolves, known for their viciousness and brutality. They used fear and violence to keep their packs in line, according to what her father had told her mother.

Guilt suddenly struck her. She hadn't called her mother in days. She'd wanted to avoid lying. Stating the truth, that she currently lived with a werewolf, under his protection, would probably send her mother into heart failure.

"What's wrong?" Anton looked concerned. It made her smile that he seemed so attuned to her feelings that he noticed her distress.

"I was just thinking about how my mother would freak out if she knew where I am and where I'm going. She's feared me meeting other shifters all my life."

"It's going to be fine," Rave offered from the seat in front of them. He turned his head and grinned. "No one is going to hurt you. You have five of the best pack fighters here. Think of us as your personal bodyguards." He winked. "Of course, only Anton gets to really hover over you."

"Rave," Anton warned softly.

264

He laughed. "What? I'm just trying to let her know she's got nothing to worry about. No way will anyone start any shit with us surrounding her."

Annoyance made Anton scowl. He squeezed Shannon's hand. "It'll be fine. My father is actually a lot nicer than my mother. My older brother mated a human and he backed Grady's decision. My mother didn't like it one bit, but then, there's not much she doesn't hate."

"You can say that again," Rave muttered. "I was forbidden to even *date* human women." He made a face at Von. "Thanks to him."

Von's grin faded. "Drop it."

Shannon glanced at Anton. He hesitated. "Von fell for a human but it didn't work out."

"I said drop it," Von demanded. "We don't discuss it, ever."

Her curiosity was piqued but obviously no one would discuss the subject. It had to be a sore topic for Von. She got the impression the human woman had hurt him.

No one spoke the rest of the drive to a secluded house surrounded by woods.

The house looked nice and very normal. Shannon wasn't sure what she'd expected to see, but a middle-class ranch house wasn't it. The van stopped and they all got out. Anton kept a tight hold on her hand.

"If you get scared," he dipped his head to peer into her eyes, "don't bolt away from me. Grab me. I'd rather hold you than have to get you down from a ceiling beam." A grin softened his words. "There are some pack members here. Not too many but I smell at least ten. There's nothing to fear, kitten. You're perfectly safe with me."

She winced. "Don't let me go, just in case. I swear I'll die of embarrassment if my instincts make me do something humiliating in front of your father."

"You're getting better at controlling it. You've done great in a van full of us."

"You're right!" That cheered her up and made her feel more confident that she wouldn't do something she'd regret.

He chuckled. "Maybe your puma is starting to think its part werewolf from adjusting to my scent."

"I don't think so. When those pride guys came into your apartment after me, I was scared but my instincts didn't respond the way they do around your kind. It really pissed me off. I wanted to flee, and tried, but I didn't go all ninja climbing skills."

Anger darkened his handsome features. "It had to be the heat you're in. It recognized them as other pumas." He snarled that last word, really getting worked up.

Shannon stared at him, unsure what had set him off, but he was getting off-the-deep-end furious.

He took a few deep breaths. "I'm jealous." He calmed, getting control of his temper. "I feel my wolf, what it wants and how it reacts to things, even when I'm in skin. It makes him wonder if the cat inside you prefers one of those assholes who kidnapped you. You're too human to control those puma genes of yours; you only react to whatever instincts come with them."

Understanding dawned and she stepped into him, gazing into his eyes. "As you pointed out, I'm too human. I can't feel a cat inside me. It's just me in here with some crazy fears that I react to. You're the only man I want, Anton."

His arm slid around her waist to pull her against him and he lifted her hand to brush a kiss over her knuckles. He smiled.

"I hate to break this up," Von interrupted softly. "We need to go inside. They're waiting."

"I know." Anton lowered her hand. "Let's go."

He released her waist, stepped back, but gripped her hand tight enough that she knew even if she panicked, she wouldn't be able to jerk free. She followed close behind him as they entered a nice living room and then walked to the back of the house to a doorway that had stairs leading downward. Rave and Von were in front of them, with Braden and Brand behind.

The couches and chairs were taken by a group of men who all turned their heads to watch them carefully. Fear shot through Shannon as she glanced at the werewolves in skin, sure all of them were exactly that, and her nose itched. She wanted to hide behind Anton when he stopped at the bottom of the stairs but she forced the urge back and stayed at his side instead.

She kept her chin up as a man suddenly walked in from a hallway at the back of the room. One look at his familiar features assured her this had to be Anton's father, but he didn't look as old as he should. He didn't even look forty.

"Dad." Rave spoke first. "I'm so sorry Mom has done this."

The man didn't look well. The black, shaggy hair that fell to his shoulders had an unkempt appearance, and dark circles made his gaze seem haunted. He focused on Shannon, and while she didn't sense any hostility, he sure didn't seem happy to see her either.

"This is her?" he rasped gruffly.

Anton tensed. "Yes. This is Shannon Alvers. She's only a quarter puma. She can't shift, Dad. She's no threat to anyone here."

"I'm Elroy Harris." He paused. "I lead the Harris Pack. First, I want to apologize for the way our pups attacked you and dragged you into our world. It shouldn't have happened. I don't condone attacking other shifters without reason, and certainly not female ones. I'm sure you were raised hearing terrible stories about our kind but we aren't brutal killers."

"Thank you. It's nice to meet you, Mr. Harris." She spoke softly around the lump that had formed in her throat. She'd never expected him to apologize to her.

268

His black eyebrow lifted. "I wouldn't call it 'nice'. We haven't exactly been friendly toward you...except for one of us." He turned his dark gaze on Anton. "It seems my son has taken a great interest in you."

"Dad..." Anton paused. "Are you okay? You look like hell."

"My mate is currently locked inside a cell, which I'm told she trapped you in earlier, and the scent of the man she killed still lingers. She really told you she planned to kill me?"

"Yes. I'm sorry. She also wants to be rid of Grady. You were both on her list."

Elroy's broad shoulders slumped. "I'm sorry too. Betrayal by the one closest to you is the hardest to take. She's put me in a hell of a situation, hasn't she? She attacked one of our children when she pulled that stunt with you and threatened the life of my oldest son." He glanced at Shannon and then back at Anton. "Did your mother know you'd marked her? I can smell it from here. You must have bitten deep."

"Yes." Anton hesitated. "She knew, and thought she'd keep me in a coma during mating heat to keep me from going feral without Shannon."

"I heard she called those pride males to take your woman." His voice deepened, his features revealed his anger, and his hands clenched at his sides. "She invited them into my territory to take what you'd claimed. She risked your life and those of all our sons by making you go after your woman. My mate plotted against our entire pack with her actions."

"I'm sorry, Dad." Von cautiously approached his father. "We love her too and this hurts us all. She's your mate, though, which makes it much worse. We've grown accustomed to the hurtful things she's capable of doing, yet she's still our mother. I wish we could take your pain."

"You can't but I appreciate it. I love my sons." He met each of their gazes. "I called our enforcers here to discuss what is to be done about this. We're too emotionally involved to make sane, logical judgments when it comes to your mother."

"What are we going to do?" Rave shoved his thumbs into the front pockets of his jeans. "We usually kill anyone who betrays the pack this severely but obviously that's out."

Elroy blinked away tears. "I could never kill my mate, despite what she planned to do to me. I wish I could forgive it, I want to, but she endangered all of you. I can't allow her to remain in a position to do it again."

Braden sniffed, his hand rose to wipe at tears on his cheeks, and he cleared his throat. "We could banish her back to her family's pack. Grandpa would make certain she doesn't cause trouble. He'd also take care of her."

Elroy glanced at the men seated around the room. One of them, a tall blond, nodded. "That's fair. The pack wouldn't object to that. No one could possibly expect you to kill your mate, Alpha."

The tension on Elroy's face lessened. "So be it then. I'll call Douglas, inform him of what his daughter has done, and tell him we're sending her to him. She's officially stripped of being my mate, a member of this pack, and banished forever for her crimes."

"Fuck," Rave sighed. "What about you, Dad? You're mated to her and it's mating heat. You can't let her go until after it passes. You'll go insane."

An older man rose from a chair. "We discussed this before you arrived. I'm going to put Elroy into an induced coma until mating heat passes. Because they're mated, he'll go through serious depression and withdrawals anyway. I'm more concerned about his grief over losing his mate. It could kill him. They've been together for so long, he might not survive the loss. I'll have to monitor him and keep him drugged regardless, so we have nothing to lose."

Anton closed his eyes, his hold on Shannon loosened, and she peered up at him. She hurt for him and the amount of pain on his features saddened her. She squeezed his hand and he opened his eyes to meet her concerned gaze. He gave her a sad smile before he broke eye contact to look at his father.

"I'll lead the pack in your absence. I don't want you to worry about anything but making it through this tough time. You're better off without a mate who would harm you or us. We all love her but she doesn't know how to love us back."

Elroy turned away, his chin dropped to his chest, and his shoulders shook. Rave wrapped an arm around him and led him down the hallway, out of sight. The older man quickly followed behind the departing pair.

Anton turned his head to glance at his brothers. "He's strong and he'll survive. Doc will take excellent care of him." His voice grew harsh. "I'm in charge for now. If anyone wants to challenge me, speak up, and we'll take this outside."

Fear jolted Shannon when she realized what he'd said. The knowledge that he might have to fight another werewolf left her feeling stark terror.

No one inside the room spoke to protest his announcement.

"Good." Anton sighed. "It's official. I'm the temporary alpha." He hesitated. "Temporary. That's the key word here. Dad will get past this and I'll concede the title back to him. We need to show a strong front for the pack. It's imperative they know everything will remain the same and it hasn't weakened us in any way."

The blond cleared his throat. "What about her, Anton? No disrespect, but it's going to cause waves with some that you've marked the enemy." The guy bit his lip. "I heard you say she can't shift and she's mainly human, but as an enforcer, it's my job to point out all possible problems."

Von stepped forward. "If it becomes a point of contention with our pack, or outside challengers who believe there's the possibility of taking the alpha position here, I'll step up. We've already discussed that scenario if Dad needed to step down, which has now happened. Its fine, Kane. One of us will lead the Harris Pack. I highly doubt anyone would want to challenge all my brothers, and that's what they would be up against." He met Anton's stare. "I phoned Grady while you and Shannon were changing clothes. He's willing to fight to help us hold the pack. We're totally united."

"I never doubted that." Anton addressed the blond. "Kane, I want you and your men to spread word that everything is taken care of and there's no cause for alarm. Perhaps it would be better if you just told them we're sharing the alpha position while our father recovers. Make sure everyone knows the entire Harris family..." He paused to glance back at Brand. "Are you united with us?"

Brand grinned. "You know I love a good fight. I've always got your backs."

Anton chuckled. "I knew that but I didn't want to speak for you." He faced Kane again. "You heard him. If they feel stupid enough to think it's a good time to challenge for lead position in the pack, it will be the last thing they ever do."

Kane grinned. "You have the support of your enforcers." He shot a glance at the other men. "I *can* speak for them, since they know I'll kill them otherwise."

A few of the men chuckled.

Anton grew serious. "I hate to do this during mating heat but for the time being, we double up in teams. We have no idea how this news will affect outsiders and there's plenty of them in town. No one goes anywhere without someone to defend their back."

"Shit," Rave groaned, walking back into the room. "Only on patrol, right?"

"No." Anton shook his head. "They may use the heat, feeling it's a perfect time to attack. Pair up at all times."

"No," Braden groaned. "Anything but that."

Rave suddenly laughed. "What's wrong, Braden? Are you afraid to have a witness around to see how little you know about females? I'll pair up with you. I'll be more than happy to give you advice if you're doing something wrong."

Shannon tugged on Anton's hand. He looked down at her. "Does that mean what I think it does? I..." Her cheeks flamed with heat and her voice lowered. "I'm not having sex with someone else inside a room with us. I can't."

He pulled her against his side and laughed. "Not in the same room but they'll be close enough that we can look out for each other if someone shows up to attack."

"You both can stay at my house," Von offered. "I've got enough bedrooms and I've got a hell of a security system. I paired up with Debbie for mating heat, and you know she won't cause any problems over Shannon's bloodlines."

274

Kane chuckled. "Debbie, huh? That's brave."

Von shrugged. "I have no interest in mating her, and we all know *she's* already set on mating someone else. I like her. She's fun and easy to get along with."

"You know Parker won't be happy about it."

"Then he shouldn't have run away. He's spending his heat with someone else, since he's not here with her. Debbie is my friend, and if he won't take care of her, I will. She's too vulnerable at this moment to trust any other male not to take advantage of the heat to mate her. She's safe with me."

Kane's humor vanished. "That's true. She's too sweet and attractive. I know a dozen males who'd try to seduce her into a mating and I'd hate to see them die when Parker finally grabs a clue. He'd kill any man who claimed her."

Shannon glanced up at Anton for clarification. He sighed. "You'll like Debbie. She's a half-breed. Some werewolves are old school and believe mating half-breeds taints the pack. Parker's family convinced him that mating her would ruin their precious heritage, and the moron left to avoid his feelings for her."

Rave cleared his throat. "I hate to break this up, but I'm starting to suffer from the heat. I feel aggressive as hell and I have a woman waiting at my place. Let's partner up and assign schedules. In another half hour, if I'm not fucking someone, there's going to be a fight."

Kane laughed. "Let's get down to business then. I'm not fucking you, man."

"You'd be the bitch, not me." Rave winked. "And you're so not my type."

Chapter Sixteen

Anton watched Shannon study his brother's guestroom and it took everything he had not to lunge at her, pin her to the bed, and tear off her clothes. His dick throbbed painfully, trapped inside his pants, aching to sink into her hot, tight body. He held back a snarl.

"You're not scenting strongly of need anymore."

She peered out the window at the view of the woods, her back to him. "I guess the hormones they gave me aren't going to have any lasting effects on me. I'll probably never go into heat that strongly again." She turned with a smile. "Isn't that great news? I'm almost normal again. I'm still achy and turned on but it's not a mindless need now."

Would I be a bastard if I disagreed? I want you hot. I'd give anything to have you burning under me again, clawing at me, unable to get enough. He kept those thoughts to himself. "I need you."

Her gaze dropped to his groin and her eyes widened. "You're in heat now. How could I not notice that before? You're as hard as a rock."

"Yeah." He had to leash his beast when it tried to spring forward. The wolf inside him howled for Shannon. Sweat broke out all over his body and he started to breathe heavily. He worried about scaring her. "My control is slipping." He winced at the harsh tone of his voice.

She reached for her shirt. "Do we have condoms? We might want to use them just in case you can't stop from biting me again. We've taken a lot of risks in the past few hours."

The memory of feeling her without them made him want to lie. Nothing had ever been as good as his bare cock riding her hot, sleek pussy as it squeezed around him. He'd always worn protection during the heat, never trusted a woman not to tempt him into mating her when his defenses were down, but Shannon wasn't just any woman. He wanted to keep her. He wanted to spill his seed deep inside her while biting into her flesh to bind them together forever.

"They're inside the nightstand. Von always keeps them stocked in all the guestrooms. He entertains out-of-town werewolves when Dad invites them here."

She removed her shirt, tossed it onto the chair in the corner, and his fists clenched at the sight of her soft, pale breasts. Her nipples probably reacted from the chill of the room instead of needing him as much as he did her. He watched her open the drawer, remove a box and set it on the edge of the nightstand. She tortured him by slowly baring every inch of her body for him to drool over. He swallowed fast, figuring she wouldn't find it sexy. His fangs elongated inside his mouth to press against the inside of his lower lip.

Shannon hesitated to peer at him with such innocence that he really felt like a bastard when all he wanted to do was bend her over and fuck her until his knees collapsed. A growl erupted. Her eyes widened and she licked her lips. It reminded him of her on her knees earlier. That had been surprising, when she'd offered to take care of his needs, and even with her lack of experience, it'd been the best blow job he'd ever gotten, despite making her stop. The memory of her mouth wrapped around him, her tongue teasing his cock, became too much.

He reached down and tore at his pants. Material ripped. He managed to scratch his thigh with a claw, realized his nails were growing as well as his dick and fangs. He closed his eyes to try to calm down and fought the urge to attack her.

"Anton?" She moved closer. "Are you okay?"

He cleared his throat. "I waited too long. Just back off. I don't want to hurt you. I'm afraid I'll take you too fast or rough."

He heard the mattress give as she got on the bed, and opened his eyes. Shannon met his gaze and really drove him insane when she scooted over to the center of the bed. Her arms lifted to grip the headboard bars with both hands, her back arched to taunt him with those luscious breasts that he wanted to suck while he fucked her. She lifted her legs and spread them apart.

The scent of warm, aroused woman slammed into him as if he'd been hit by a two-by-four. His gaze fastened on her pussy and he saw the glistening folds of a woman who wanted him.

279

He hit the bed before he realized he'd moved. *Keep your skin*, he silently yelled when his wolf shoved against him from inside, wanting to take her as much as he did. He crouched on all fours with his face over her spread thighs. He felt torn between wanting to bury his face there or his cock, which screamed for relief.

He glanced up to meet her eyes and saw the trust there. She showed no sign of fear though he knew he probably looked pretty terrifying. It calmed him enough to make the correct choice. She wasn't ready to take him in full heat.

His head lowered, the scent of her making him whimper, and he couldn't stop salivating. She wouldn't see that but she'd certainly feel it. He lifted a hand and paused, horrified at his claws protruding an inch from his fingertips. He couldn't touch her delicate skin or he'd tear her up.

He glanced back at her, unable to speak. Another whimper came from him. He knew hell. He was would die before he hurt Shannon but he wouldn't survive if he didn't fuck her soon.

Shannon took deep breaths to remain calm despite knowing how close Anton appeared to losing all control. She wasn't going to point out that he now had soft black hair on the sides of his face, as if he'd grown sideburns. The color of his eyes had also turned pitch black but other than that, he looked human. Then she saw him staring at his hand with a look of frustration that bordered on horror. She followed his gaze and saw the problem.

280

She released the headboard and spread her thighs wider. She only hesitated for a second before reaching down to spread her folds to fully expose her pussy to him.

"Is this what you want?"

He snarled — the sound excited more than scared her. He made that soft, pained noise again and tore his gaze from hers to lower to her sex. His fangs showed but he carefully pressed his mouth against her. His tongue rasped against her clit and she closed her eyes when desire flared inside her body as he took one long lick that made her moan. He paused and did it again.

His tongue moved faster, furiously lapping at her, applying more pressure when he nuzzled against her as if he couldn't get close enough. It drove her passion higher until she removed her hands from her pussy to fist a handful of his hair. She had to tug roughly to get him to release her. His head jerked up and he growled at her, his displeasure clear.

"Fuck me," she demanded. "I want you now; we're both hurting to come. I won't mind if you're rough. I want you to be."

He lifted up, the anger easing from his features, and she didn't take it personally that she'd pissed him off. She understood mating heat now that she'd suffered it firsthand. It was a mindless need — a clawing, painful, gut-wrenching obsession to have sex that left little room for thought.

281

He didn't touch her with his hands as he climbed over her. His intense gaze locked with hers and she didn't try to kiss him. His fangs probably wouldn't have made that possible without pain. Her hand lowered and she didn't have to look away from his eyes to find his cock. Her fingers curled around hot, incredibly thick male. His eyes narrowed and he groaned and tipped his head back. His body trembled inches above hers.

She lifted her leg to place one heel on his ass, used her other leg to brace on the bed, and maneuvered her body under his to guide the crown of his cock against the entrance to her pussy. He held still, his entire body rigid, and she knew he was allowing her to take control. She also acknowledged how much inner strength he possessed to fight back the urge to take her.

She heard material rip and jerked her head to the side. His hands fisted the bedding, his claws shredding the material.

"Anton? Take me. You won't hurt me."

He refused to look at her, so she lifted her hips, wiggled into perfect position, and tugged on his shaft gently to lure him to enter her.

"Fuck me." She released his cock and grabbed his ass to dig in her fingernails.

Anton lowered his face, their gazes fused, and he slowly dropped down on her. Sweat beaded his brow and upper lip as he sank into her pussy slowly.

She remembered then that they hadn't grabbed a condom, but she didn't want to stop.

She moaned as her vaginal walls were stretched to the point of near pain as he entered her. His cock seemed bigger, thicker, and definitely harder than before. Hot too. She could relate, since she wondered if they'd ignite the bed. She burned for him. Her hips bucked.

That broke his control. His hips slammed against her spread thighs, drove him balls deep into her pussy, and she cried out. "Yes!"

She barely had time to take a breath before he came down on top of her completely, pinned her securely to the bed under him, and his hips started to jackhammer fast and furiously against her. She squeezed her eyes closed, clung to him, and drowned in ecstasy as one unrestrained, sexy Anton fucked her with desperation born from pure lust.

She didn't care that the headboard slammed loudly against the wall, the pounding nothing compared to her racing heartbeat, her ragged breathing, or the sheer rapture he created. He kept up the furious pace of thrusting deep, nearly sliding out of her completely, only to slam into her again. Sensitive nerve endings seemed to overtake her entire body until the sensory overload of pleasure nearly became too powerful.

Her body shook, her vaginal walls clamped around Anton, and she started to climax. A powerful orgasm coursed throughout her body. She watched Anton with pure love.

Anton howled out his own release when he threw his head back. His hips seized and he trembled violently against her.

He suddenly snapped his head down until their noses nearly touched. His black gaze was so intense she felt she could read his mind. He opened his mouth, sharp fangs showing. His attention shifted from her eyes to somewhere lower and to the right of her jaw. She knew what he intended to do.

He lunged for her shoulder and she released him to grab a fistful of hair when his teeth touched her skin.

"No!" she yelled. "Don't!" Her other hand rose to grip another handful of his hair.

Anton's body continued to twitch and she could feel hot jets of his semen filling her. Her vaginal muscles helped it along by milking him with the aftershocks of her climax. His teeth didn't bite into her though, just held her in their grip tight enough that the points of his fangs dug in slightly, to let her know how close he came to puncturing skin.

She tugged on him. "Don't. Let go, baby. Don't bite me."

His jaw relaxed, the pressure eased, and he suddenly turned his face away.

Anton panted and then shoved his face into the bedding next to her head. He groaned and she felt more of his semen fill her. He seemed to keep coming, and she released his hair to wrap her arms around his shoulders. Her hands caressed his upper back, her legs wrapped around his hips tighter, to hold him, and finally both of their bodies seemed to relax.

They lay there until their breathing returned to normal. Anton allowed her to soothe him and just enjoy touching him. She knew she'd never grow tired of exploring his body with her fingertips. She could feel his cock, still rigid inside her, but he'd warned her that would be a side effect of mating heat. He'd remain aroused, ready for sex, and she silently promised to give him as much as he craved. She smiled. It would be her pleasure.

"You okay?" He muffled the words.

"I'm great. Want to go another round?"

His body tensed but then relaxed again. He took a deep breath before he pushed up enough to stare down at her. He studied her eyes and she saw something in his that she couldn't understand. Sadness.

"I'm sorry."

"For what? You didn't hurt me, Anton. That was amazing. I'm up for the rest of mating heat with you. Do you want me again?"

"I always want you, though the heat fades a little between bouts of sex."

His eyes changed as she watched—the black receded to show the pretty brown again. The faint hair on his cheeks disappeared and his fangs slid up into a perfectly straight row of white, normal-looking teeth. It amazed her how he could do that and she had to admit it was impressive.

"I nearly mated you."

"I know. I didn't want you to do something you'd regret." She tried to hide her disappointment. "Trust me. I'm never going to forget losing my mind when I was filled with hormones. I hope I didn't hurt you when I pulled your hair."

"You didn't. You had to do it to stop me. I wouldn't have regretted it, Shannon. I told you we needed to talk. That's what I wanted us to discuss." He hesitated. "Would you have hated me if I'd bitten you?"

"No. Never." Her heart started to race. "What are you trying to say?"

"I don't want to lose you, Shannon. When mating heat passes, I don't want to let you go. I'm a werewolf, I realize we're going to face a lot of shit since my pack won't be happy with a part-puma living with me, but I don't give a damn. Will you consider staying with me?"

Tears filled her eyes, momentarily blinding her, and she had to fight them back. Anton softly cursed.

"I'm sorry. I should have kept my mouth closed. It's too soon. Will you at least give us a chance? We'll have time to get to know each other better by the time I go out of heat. All I ask is for you to keep an open mind that maybe you could get past what I am and care about me the way I do you."

"I don't have to do that."

He winced. "Okay." His gaze darted anywhere but at her face. "We'll use condoms. I'll put on a muzzle if that's what it takes to prevent me from biting you. I want to mate you but I'd never force it."

"Anton?"

"It's okay. You're human. You need more time." He finally met her gaze. "I'm not crazy or a lunatic. I just know I want to be with you, I love you, and I'd like to spend the rest of my life as your mate. I want to be honest so you know where I stand." He paused. "I'm hoping you'll fall in love with me. I'm going to warn you now…" A smile bowed his lips. "I'm not going to play fair. I'll do anything to convince you that I'm your perfect mate."

More tears flowed but she didn't try to force them back anymore. "I only stopped you from biting me because I thought you might be out of control. I don't need you to convince me of anything. I love you."

His gaze widened.

"Do you think I'd let just any guy take me to bed?" She grinned. "I love you, Anton. I don't want to leave you. I never want to lose what we have." She cocked her head to the side and positioned her body enough to elevate one shoulder to offer it to him. "I'm yours for the taking if you want me."

His sexy eyes darkened. "I want you, kitten."

Shannon's chest started to vibrate and she began to purr — without his hands stroking her body. Her eyes widened with surprise but Anton grinned.

"It sounds as if you might have a bit more cat inside you than you knew. I'm taking that for a yes from her, too."

"This is so embarrassing," she groaned. She cleared her throat and the purring ceased. "You bring out so much inside me that I've never experienced before."

"We'll work it out." He chuckled. "We've got time. Lots of it." He withdrew his cock from her and moaned. "I always hate separating us."

"Then why are you getting up?"

He sat back on his heels. "Roll over. This is easier to do doggy style." He chuckled at his joke. "Besides, I've already scarred you. I want to keep it to a minimum when I mate you. I'll bite over where I already have."

Surprise held her still. "You want to mate now?"

288

All traces of humor erased from his features. "Yes. Do you want to wait?"

"No." She rolled over and moved to her hands and knees, threw her hair out of the way, and smiled at him over her shoulder. She wiggled her ass. "Do it."

He lifted to his knees. "I love you, Shannon. I will protect you with my life, make it my first priority to always see to your happiness, and I pledge my eternal love to you."

His words touched her so much she battled tears. "I promise to love you forever too. I'd die for you as well, and I'll do anything to make you happy."

His fangs slid down as she watched and he nudged her thighs farther apart with his knee, gently. "You're mostly human, and I know what humans consider the ultimate commitment. Will you marry me?"

She laughed. "I'm about to let you bite me. What's a wedding compared to that? Of course I will, but something really small and fun. Nothing big or dramatic, okay? I figure we'll face enough stress when your pack finds out you've mated me."

He chuckled. "Good." His gaze dropped to her curvy ass. "You're so hot. You have no idea what you do to me."

She twisted a little to get a look at his stiff cock and grinned. "I can see, and I do know. You do the same to me." She wiggled her ass again. "Make me happy."

Anton adjusted his legs outside of hers and nudged her wet folds with his cock. He entered her slowly, her pleasure instant at the feel of him stretching her vaginal walls until he slid into her deep and she moaned. He didn't move once he got into that position.

His voice turned gruff. "I love you, kitten."

"I love you too, wolf."

He laughed, wrapped his body over hers, and caged her under him. "I'll try not to hurt you when I bite. Just hold still when I do. I don't want to tear your skin any more than I have to. I need to stay locked inside you to cement our mating. I want a strong bond formed between us."

She met his gaze. "So do I. You won't hurt me. I trust you."

He kept her gaze as he started to slowly move, thrusting in and out of her. She gripped the bedding to brace her body and pushed back to meet his hips. Ecstasy filled her with every motion. Desire burned hotter and brighter as they moved against each other, building to a frenzy of motion. Anton's arm wrapped around her waist to lock her against him and he hammered her harder and faster.

Shannon had to look away, her head lowered, and she screamed as the climax hit. Anton snarled and she tried not to tense when his sharp fangs pierced her skin. She cried out again, the pain minimal compared to the second climax his bite sent throughout her body.

He groaned, his body jerked against hers as he started to come, and she could feel him filling her with his warm release. It seemed to go on forever. His mouth suckled her shoulder, his warm tongue against the curve of it as he held her inside his mouth during the mini aftershocks of the intense sex they'd just shared.

He finally released her from his teeth. His tongue lapped at her bite mark and she chuckled. "That kind of tickles."

He paused. "I'm yours now, and you're mine. We're mated."

She turned her head until their gazes met. "I love you."

"I love you too."

Epilogue

Three weeks later

Shannon laughed and ducked under Anton's arm when he lunged at her. "You missed me."

He grinned. "In more ways than one. I couldn't stop thinking about you while I visited my dad. The past two hours seemed as though a week passed. I want you."

She paused by their brand-new bed to grin at him. "Come and get me then." She lifted the hem of her skirt enough to show him her bare thighs. "Want to guess what I'm not wearing?"

His sexy gaze lowered. "Want to guess where I'm about to put my face to find out?"

She inched the skirt higher to reveal more thigh. "How is your father?"

"He's growing stronger." He tore his shirt over his head. "Our doctor assures us he'll make it. He should be able to take the pack back in less than a month."

"And your mother?"

"My grandfather has her. He'll make sure she isn't able to cause any more trouble." He bent to remove his boots. "Enough talk." He opened the snap of his jeans. "I've done my family duty today. Now it's all about us."

"I like that." She licked her lips. "I love it when you look at me like that."

He shoved his jeans down his thighs and pure lust gripped Shannon at seeing him completely stripped bare. Anton had to be the sexiest male who ever walked the earth — and he was her mate.

"I'm about to love you a hell of a lot."

She backed up until her legs touched the edge of their new bed. "Sounds fun."

He stalked toward her and paused just inches away. He surprised her when he suddenly dropped to his knees and grabbed one of her legs. He lifted it, careful not to make her lose her balance, and settled the curve of her knee over his broad shoulder. His gaze lowered to her pussy in front of his face. A soft growl rumbled from his throat.

"No panties, kitten?" He gripped her skirt, shoved it higher, out of the way, and leaned in. "And you're wet. Have I mentioned how I love your scent and taste? I'm addicted to you." He opened his mouth and licked her clit.

Shannon grabbed for one of the bedposts with one hand and held her skirt out of his way with the other. "That feels so good."

He lapped at her and the vibration started inside her chest at the pleasure his mouth created. The purrs coming from her were something she had grown accustomed to. She only experienced them when Anton made love to her or caressed her after sex. It seemed to turn him on more, so she'd stopped trying to resist the urge when it struck.

He suddenly stopped teasing her clit and she met his gaze when he grinned at her.

"What?"

"You're my *purrfect* mate." He mimicked the sounds she made when he said it.

She laughed. "I guess I am. You're a *grrrreat* mate," she growled at him.

He suddenly rose, chuckling. Her leg over his shoulder caused her to fall back onto the bed as Anton came down on top of her. "We're a hell of a pair, aren't we?"

Her hands caressed his face. "We're purrfect."

He laughed again. "Ready to purr for me, kitten?" He nudged her with his cock.

"Ready to howl for me, baby?"

His mouth came down on hers. Shannon wrapped her legs around his waist and slid her fingers into his silky hair as the kiss deepened. She'd take that as a yes.

Made in the USA
Columbia, SC
23 May 2022

60831775R00176